REVEALING MARISA

BOOK TWO OF THE SACRIFICIAL FORTUNES SERIES

KIMMY L. DAVIS

Revealing Marisa is a work of fiction. Names, characters, places, and incidents are the product of the author's imagination or are used fictitiously. Any resemblance to actual events, locales, or persons, living or dead, is entirely coincidental.

DEDICATION

For Emma, Noah, and Lilah with love.

TABLE OF CONTENTS

ACKNOWLEDGMENTS

I am very thankful to my sisters, Kelly and Krissy, for always reading my work. Special thanks to my editor Diane Darst and my publisher Jeffrey Rogers and the White Lion Group. Thanks to friends like Lisa, Ben and Jenny S. for their incredible support. Thanks to my students who help keep me inspired and the readers who cared enough to write me reviews! I hope you love the story of Marisa and Ethan.

Chapter One

The bitter smoke suffocated her and burned her throat. Hand to mouth, she launched the cup of water at the fire burning in the antique silver bowl. What was she thinking? She'd been secretly working on spells for two years now with the help of her grandmother, who would never have mixed Angelica root with Damiana. Walking back to the bathroom for a second cup, she sighed, the urgency of the situation relieved. Ashes smoldered and she had no idea what to do about the smell. Air freshener wouldn't cover this mess.

She dialed her closest friend, Beige, while waving her other hand uselessly through the thick, curling smoke. Marisa had met Beige last year around Halloween. She had thought she'd never be accepted for herself at Garrison Prep, but while Beige looked like all the others on the outside, on the inside she was special. Beige had a gift. She could interpret the tarot and make connections with the spirit world. She worked a few times a week with Madame Clairee from Fortunes, a local witch shop, on her skills, and Madame Clairee made it clear that she believed Beige had a "destiny".

What Beige also had, that Marisa lacked, was a boyfriend. Madame Clairee's son, the beautiful Sam, had fallen hard for Beige from their very first meeting, and after he helped save Beige's life when her then best friend Sara secretly drugged her, Beige was more into him than ever. There was more to it, of course. He also helped Beige connect to her favorite aunt who had just passed away, and Marisa knew that weighed as heavily with Beige as him having saved her life.

She threw the phone on her bed leaving a familiar "call me" message for Beige and looked around at the chaos she had created. She packed her supplies into the black shoeboxes she stored in the back of her closet where her mother was sure not to look.

"I wish someone would save me from this family," she huffed as she pushed a box to the back of the closet, "or from this school," thinking of the long halls of blank faces. She slid down against the wall and hugged a pillow against her chest as she closed her eyes and fought to hold back tears. "It's all a lie. Why can't they just love me for me?"

Marisa's parents were sweet people who went to church every week and volunteered in every city they'd lived in. They raised her carefully and sent her to really good schools. To say she was sheltered would be an understatement. Nothing she knew about anything worth dreaming about came from them, and she didn't only mean sex and stuff. They hadn't given her any goals beyond to do the right thing and believe in Jesus. To her parents, she was a meek and timid little girl.

That's what she loved about her friendship with Beige. When Marisa was with Beige she felt wild and confident. She wanted to change the world with her magic and to feel love and desire for another human being, like she saw in Beige's eyes when her friend looked at Sam. Marisa was almost 17 and had never even been on a date. She'd had crushes over the years but they always seemed to lead to embarrassment, so she'd stopped sharing. Beige had tried to get the name of her latest crush out of her, but since Marisa didn't know how Beige would react if she knew the secret crush was Ethan Martos, she kept it to herself.

"Maybe I should just tell her. There's no way it's going to come true, so she can't be too offended. Besides, he wasn't the one out to hurt her anyway. He didn't even know what Sara was doing." She heard the defensiveness in her own voice, and was quick to remind herself it didn't matter. She didn't have a chance with a boy like him to begin with.

Pulled from the inner argument by her favorite ringtone, she got up from the floor, plopped across the bed, and immediately began to tell Beige all about the mess she'd made. Holding the phone a foot away from her ear, she heard Beige laughing at her.

"Not again, Risa! You should buy air freshener in bulk. Seriously, why are you still doing all this at home? You know the witch shop would be safer."

"I know, I know," she moaned. "I should never have mixed Angelica root with Damiana, but I got distracted and wasn't paying attention, and before I knew it I was eating smoke!"

"Ha! Distracted? I can't believe anything short of a banshee could stop you when you're casting a spell, or I guess you were mixing a potion, right? I'm a tarot girl. Well, tarot and dead aunts." She paused before continuing, "Still, not up on my witch words."

"I love the fact that you even try, Beige. You're one of the only people in the world besides Grandma Emma that knows who I really am and actually likes me." Marisa took a breath. She paused, almost afraid to say it, like it would disappear or not be true anymore. "You're my best friend, Beige."

"I love you too, Ris."

Right back at her, it hadn't even taken Beige a second to think about it. She showed her feelings effortlessly. No fear, she just put it out there, not worried what anyone else thought. She was so sure of herself and the fact that her love would be accepted. Marisa felt the longing churn in her stomach. Why couldn't her life be that easy?

"I've got to go deal with this smell before Mom and Dad get back from prayer group. Talk to you later, K?"

She put down the pink receiver of the antiquated phone her parents had given her when she was six, a princess phone for a princess. In the eyes of her parents, Marisa was a perfect child, the operative word being child. Here she was, a junior in high school, and her parents refused to let her drive anywhere but to take her grandmother on errands.

"It's not that we don't trust YOU, sweetie," her mom had explained patiently. "We can't control everyone else on the road, and there are so many dangerous drivers these days. Did you see that video on texting and driving they showed after church last week? So scary." She had looked straight into Marisa's eyes while she shook her head. "We just don't want to lose you."

Conveniently, her grandmother frequently needed to see Madame Clairee at Fortunes. That's how she had been lucky enough to become friends with Beige. She'd never had a real best friend before. Most of the people in her grade schools had been nice, but she always felt like they were laughing at her behind her back or they wanted her to be so much more than she really was. When she got to Garrison Prep it was easier to not try, and she'd made it through all of freshman, and the beginning of sophomore, year without anyone paying attention.

That day at Fortunes was the day Marisa truly felt her life begin. At first, she didn't want to hope that Beige might be for real, but she couldn't ignore her gut which was sending her pretty clear signals that this girl was genuinely interested in what she was saying. Against all reason she made an intuitive move and reached out to Beige again, and the results had been worth it.

As a blossoming witch, Marisa totally believed in fate. No doubt about it, larger forces than herself had brought Beige and the wonderful family she had created at Fortunes into her life. A talented witch who was patiently teaching her the craft, a bubbly little girl who seemed like the little sister she never had, a handsome and caring older brother figure who would lay down his life not only for Beige but for Marisa if she needed him: how much luckier could she have gotten? It was fate that made Garrison her new hometown a few years ago, and fate that the more confident she became in these core relationships, the more confident she was becoming in other areas of her life as well.

The face of Ethan Martos flashed in her mind.

She caught a glimpse of herself in the mirror. Her green eyes rimmed with light colored lashes that matched the red of her hair crinkled with a smile she couldn't suppress when she thought of him. She noticed her freckles. 'We couldn't be more different if we tried," she thought aloud while she wiped the soot from the silver bowl and lovingly placed it in the last black shoebox with her sealed her bags of herbs. "He's beautiful, confident, popular, and athletic. He's totally himself and loved for it and I'm not… I'm just not."

In Marisa's eyes Ethan was perfect. 6'1" and senior captain of the Garrison Prep soccer team, his curly brown locks were a bit longer than what her mother thought a good boy's hair should be. But if you looked him in those dreamy dark brown eyes, you could tell he truly was a good boy. Last year there had been some debate over that when Beige had suspected him of putting drugs in her drink on a date, but the culprit turned out to be the girl he started dating later, Sara. Even when he found out what Sara did to Beige, he'd tried to help her. He tried to get her to see a counselor, and when that failed, he'd gone to her parents.

If anyone other than Ethan Martos had accused their daughter of the things he had, they would have kicked him out of their home. But Ethan was Ethan. He oozed honesty the way Sam oozed sex appeal. Sara's parents didn't think twice about sending her in for psychiatric treatment. Rumor had it that Ethan was thinking they'd get back together when she came home. He'd told a friend he thought everyone deserved a second chance, but Sara wasn't as forgiving as Ethan.

Now that she was home, they still ran in the same crowd, but rarely spoke. She rarely spoke to any of them. Beige had hoped for an apology. Marisa was one of the few people who knew how much the whole thing had truly hurt her. Beige had cried over the lost friendship and prayed that when Sara came home she would be her old self again.

Marisa thought Beige was a little naïve. She didn't tell her that she thought Sara was her old self to begin with.

She picked up her measuring spoons and rinsed them off in the bathroom sink. "It's funny all the ways people hide who they really are," she said as she packed the spoons and herbs with the bowl and carried the box to the back of the closet. With a grunt of regret she closed the double doors on her supplies and herself. "Back to real life," she sighed.

Chapter Two

The art room at Garrison Prep was a long rectangular space lined with yellow pinewood tables and stools. Finished projects hung on the strips that surrounded the tables. Currently the display consisted of figure drawings by various students in the advanced drawing class. Marisa stared longingly at images of Ethan posed as Rodin's "The Thinker". The sinuous curve of his back as he hunched in deep thought was totally amazing. She felt butterflies in her stomach thinking that the real Ethan was merely seats away, but she wouldn't dare glance in his direction.

From the outside most people would see a contradiction in the school's most popular athlete posed as an intellectual, but Marisa knew that Ethan was as smart as he was athletically gifted. She'd shared many AP classes with him over the years and was always impressed by the seriousness with which he approached his school work. He never complained or talked about a teacher. He just did his work, and did it well.

She still didn't understand what he was doing in her art class. It wasn't that he didn't have any talent. The drawings she'd seen of his weren't half bad, but she had never heard him speak about art or even talk to people who took art classes. To be honest, she didn't like the fact that he was there. Sure, she had a major crush on him, but he made her nervous and art was the place where, up until now, she'd been able to relax.

When he was in class she couldn't focus or take her time on her sketches. An arm that would normally take her an hour would be done in 15 minutes, and it wouldn't be her best work. There was no hope of concentration. Still, the thrill of having him in the room for one more class was almost worth the deterioration of her grade.

She looked back to the front of the room where Laura Sykes stretched her arms skyward, holding a pose that looked like a child reaching for a star. Putting charcoal to paper, Marisa slowly let the black stub follow the path of her eyes up Laura's arm, to the tips of her outstretched fingers. The feeling of something beautiful being just out of reach was a familiar one to Marisa, and she sighed as melancholy replaced excitement.

"The proportion is slightly off, Marisa." The voice of Mrs. Whelan sounded behind her. "You seem to be having more trouble this semester than last. Do you find the human figure more challenging than landscape work?" Mrs. Whelan let her scarlet-rimmed glasses slide down her pert nose as her almond shaped eyes searched for a reason why her star student was struggling.

Marisa, extremely aware of Ethan's presence and the stillness of the classroom, wanted to do anything but answer and draw his attention her way. How embarrassing could this get? She was being called out in front of everyone. Of course, she knew that wasn't Mrs. Whelan's intention, the woman was like a second mom to her, but it was what it felt like all the same.

"I do, yes, Mrs. Whelan. It's not clicking for me, I guess. Maybe you have some advice?"

"I'd love to give you some pointers, Marisa. Why don't you stay after class if you don't have to be anywhere and I'll teach you how to avoid what I think is giving you the most trouble." She could feel Ethan's gaze shift and turn in her direction. She was sure her face was crimson. Unless Mrs. Whelan could tell her how to avoid Mr. Curly Haired Soccer Boy, she didn't think anything would help.

"I can do that, sure, Mrs. Whelan." Why did she have to sound like such a little girl when she spoke? Being polite was something her parents had impressed upon her from birth, but sometimes it just made her sound so uncool. She should deal with the fact that she was uncool and embrace her inner idiot. Or, maybe not. The bell had rung and Ethan was walking in her direction, curiously lacking his books.

"So you're having trouble with the human figure too, huh?"

Mesmerized by his, she forced an "Uh huh."

"Mrs. Whelan already asked me to stay after last class, but I couldn't because of soccer. I said I'd stay today instead, so you'll have company." He dropped to the empty stool at her side.

Mrs. Whelan glanced their way and made a "just a second" sign with her finger before walking out.

Marisa was alone with her dream man for the first time since their walk last year. The walk when she told him about Sara and asked for his help. The walk when he didn't know he'd been under a spell.

"I'm sorry about you and Sara," she said before she thought it through.

He looked at her a little funny, "Thanks, I guess. It's been a while now, you know. I'm fine."

"Yes, but it had to hurt, and it was a pretty big deal. I know you wanted to stay with her so…" she trailed off, not knowing how to get out of the awkwardness.

He made eye contact and took a deep breath. "When we took that walk last year, Marisa, it was one of the hardest conversations I've ever had. I still don't know why I believed you about Sara. The things you were telling me were so far off from the girl I knew. They didn't make sense, but there was something about you that made me sure you were telling me the truth. I liked that about you. I still do. You can tell me the truth now too. You're not sorry I broke up with Sara."

Marisa gulped. Could he possibly know that she was into him? She'd been so careful to not give him any signs. "Ethan…" but he cut her off before she could get a word out.

"I'm not judging you, Marisa. I'd have vengeful thoughts about Sara too, if I were you. I know you and Beige don't like her, and I know you didn't think I should have stayed with her."

A sense of relief flooded through her. and she realized she had been holding her breath.

"Oh, yeah, right. Yes, it was hard to understand." She paused and continued on with more grace, "But I thought it was really right of you to want to give her a second chance. You have a good soul, Ethan."

His eyes searched hers for a second before he got up and walked back to his table. He put his drawing supplies away and picked up his books. There was discomfort in his voice when he spoke. "Tell Whelan I had to get going, OK? Late for conditioning…must have forgot." He scooted past her quickly and Marisa was left standing alone with her figure drawing.

"I guess it's not only the human figure I'm having trouble with," she thought to herself. "It seems to be all humans."

Chapter Three

Madame Clairee laughed loudly at Beige's interpretation of the reading before them.

"While I am sure there is always a possibility of the Jones Brothers breaking up, Beige, I would appreciate it if you would keep the news from Lilah. It would devastate her."

"Marisa!" Beige said.

Madame Clairee looked up to see her "third daughter" enter the colorful reading room decorated in red and gold jewel tones. She thought for a moment how her life had been full with Lilah and Sam. She hadn't needed more, but since the addition of Beige and Marisa, their daily life had been an explosion of excitement, friendship, and love. She loved the two young women as if they were her own, and truth be told, she hoped one day Beige might be. That is if her son Sam had half a brain to hold onto a good thing.

Not right away, of course. She was proud of what Sam was doing at the local community college, pursuing his degree in Criminal Justice. A job as a police officer was work where Sam could change the world, and with a psychic mother and sister, tarot reading girlfriend, and witch "sister", there was no way he'd be caught off guard or harmed.

"Come in, sweetie! I didn't expect you until later. Why didn't you just come with Beige?"

Marisa looked sheepishly at Beige and Clairee, "Mrs. Whelan wanted me to stay after to work on my art, but I told her something came up. I wasn't in the mood."

Clairee and Beige exchanged glances and spoke in unison, "Sit."

"Shuffle the cards, Marisa," Beige ordered as she slid the handsome deck trimmed in gold leaf across the table.

"These are gorgeous, Beige. Are they new? I've never seen them before."

"No distracting me, Ris. Sit and shuffle."

She shrugged her shoulders and rolled her eyes before collapsing onto the comfortable couch lined with pillows. "I don't want you delving into my soul right now, Beige."

"Nonsense," Clairee answered. "You obviously need advice; your aura is screaming for attention. Let us help. It'll be fun."

Marisa doubted the fun part, but she didn't question that they could help her. What would the cards reveal if she asked about Ethan? She wasn't ready to let Clairee and Beige in on all that was going on in her heart. She noticed them exchanging looks again.

"What? Why do you two keep looking at each other like that? Do you have some secret you don't want to tell me?" she asked.

"No, do you?" Beige shot back, smiling mischievously.

Oh God. They knew. She knew they knew, and she wasn't even psychic, just a plain old witch. But how much did they know? Did they know this crush had been going on for the past year or did they think it was new? Did they know she wrote his name in her journal and dreamed about him every night?

"Having psychic friends is such an invasion of privacy." She crossed her arms and closed her eyes.

"Come on, Risa, shuffle the cards. It'll be fun. All the practice I got today was a reading for Lilah about tweeny bopper music. Give me some mature love to work with." Beige laughed.

"Eeeew, that sounds like you're talking about Grandma Emma. I don't even want to picture it." She shook her head to clear the disturbing image, which unfortunately was all too easy to picture since her grandmother had been seeing old Mr. Datillo from the retirement home. She picked up the cards, absentmindedly shuffling as in her mind she replaced the old people with Ethan's angelic face.

"That's enough, Risa. Come back to earth now." Beige took the cards from her hand and asked her to cut them three times with her left hand. "It's the hand that's closest to your heart, you know." She winked. Beige actually winked at her. That had to mean she was OK with this, right?

Marisa wasn't sure she wanted this reading. What if it was bad or it said there was no way, no how, ever, that Ethan Martos would like her? She wasn't ready to find that out and let her crush go. She reached out to grab the cards back, but Beige was already laying out the spread. A simple three card spread. Past, present, future, she couldn't get too much out of that, could she?

"Courage, the Star reversed, and the High Priestess, all major arcana cards. This is a big deal, huh?"

Madame Clairee's eyes roved the cards Beige had flipped and felt her heart fall. She looked at the card representing the present. The Star reversed was a sad card. Not because anything bad would happen, but because it indicated a lack of self-esteem and not believing in yourself. Clairee had hoped that this past year had changed some of that for Marisa, but it was suddenly obvious to her in the pit of her stomach it hadn't. She looked into Marisa's nervous, frightened eyes. The poor thing wanted so badly to be loved for who she was. What she hadn't found yet was a way to love herself. She sat back to see how Beige would interpret the reading.

"Courage is in the past. I think this probably takes us back to last year when you helped us by talking to Ethan. Putting that spell on him was a risky thing to do. If he'd found out, I don't think he would have understood, given his views on magic. But he didn't find out, and you made a connection with him through your courage."

Marisa winced at Beige's reference to Ethan's views on magic. She didn't really know what he thought, because no one had ever asked him, but he had been with Sara, who was very clear in her belief that everything connected to the witch shop was evil. He also was the poster boy for Garrison Prep, leading mission trips and bible studies. There was no way his views could be good.

"The present is interesting." Beige continued. "I think this represents you. You don't believe in yourself. You honestly don't think there's any way to win his heart, do you?" Beige stopped and looked into Marisa's eyes that were filled with shame. She scooted closer and wrapped an arm around her friend who had become her sister.

"Hey, it's OK…we know how wonderful you are. You just need some time to catch up. You're magnificent, Marisa...as a friend, a person, and a witch. 100% perfect the way you are."

"I second that." Clairee came over and put her arm around Marisa's other shoulder. "You are a special person with a special purpose and don't you ever forget it. Despite this present lack of self-esteem, you may notice that the card of the future is the High Priestess."

"That's really good," Beige said, "It's a woman who uses her intuition and the occult powers for good. You're coming into your own. Maybe Ethan will notice your new confidence if you find a way to let it bloom?"

"There's no maybe about it, Marisa. I've had a distinct vision regarding this reading, you and Ethan. You will be together, but it will be totally your choice whether you stay together. You hold all the cards." Clairee smiled and stood. "I need some chai tea. Sodas for you girls? "

Clairee left in a whoosh. A small voice from the other room called out as she followed her mother into the kitchen, "He likes you

Marisa….he really does." Giggles followed and a second voice could be heard with Lilah.

"Who likes her? Who is she? What are you talking about?"

Lilah appeared in the doorway, her jet black curls tied up in big pink ribbon. "I don't know if I should say…can I tell her, Marisa?"

Marisa looked at the two giddy eleven year-olds. It was nice to see Lilah with a friend. Marisa thought back, trying to remember if friendship had ever been that easy at her age.

"I don't see why not. What are the chances she'll spill my secret to a boy she doesn't even know."

"Oh, she knows him!" Lilah said. "Her older brother is his friend. He was at her house yesterday after soccer."

The little blond named Katie let out a squeal.

"No way! Ethan? She likes Ethan? And Ethan likes her, too? How do you know?" Katie's pitch got higher with each new question.

Lilah thought for a moment. She had to be careful about revealing too much of her family's special talents. Garrison was full of believers, but not necessarily in what her family practiced. She liked Katie and wanted to keep her as a friend. "We don't know for sure, but we think he does. Who wouldn't like Marisa? She's gorgeous."

"You are pretty, Marisa. I love your red hair, and your eyelashes are so long. He probably does like you. I heard him telling Tommy about some girl, but he didn't say her name."

Marisa covered her eyes with her hand. "Oh God, could this get any worse? Help me, Beige."

Beige looked at both the girls and spoke firmly, "Lilah, Katie, this is what we call a life or death secret. It's a secret of the sisterhood, like the movie, OK? Only true friends reveal the deepest parts of their hearts to each other. Marisa has trusted us with something sacred. We should make a vow that we won't reveal this secret. If we do, we accept that something truly horrible will happen to us."

She noticed Katie shifting back and forth. Maybe she'd laid it on a little too thick. "Well, not horrible, but something we wouldn't like….like maybe the Jones Brothers would break up."

Fear filled the faces of both Lilah and Katie as they quickly put their hands on the table, one on top of the other. Beige put hers on top of theirs, and Marisa's went last.

"We swear by the bonds of sisterhood not to reveal the identity of Marisa's love," Lilah said out loud, followed by a "definitely" from Katie.

A strange energy filled the room.

"Well there you have it, Ris. Your secret's safe as can be!"

Chapter Four

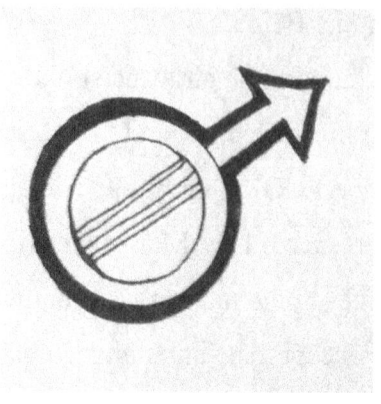

Sam sat in his car outside Garrison Prep waiting for cheerleading practice to let out. If anyone noticed him they would think he was just a boy waiting for his girlfriend. No one would know he was really an angry stalker making sure his girlfriend's life would never be in danger again. But no one noticed because no one cared, and he was able to keep an eye out for Sara without any interference. Sam knew that he couldn't be sure what she was up to without talking to her, but after his experience with Beige's dead aunt last year, he had embraced his psychic abilities and felt pretty confident that if Sara was thinking about harming Beige in any way, he would pick up on it.

He watched the group of girls, all eerily alike in looks and movement, exit the side door of the gym. Sara was their center, her short pixie style haircut now shoulder length and pulled back in a pony. Amazing. She went on with her daily life like last year never happened, still popular and admired. Her friends hadn't known the real reason for her psychiatric treatment, and he was sure Sara had come up with some reason they would secretly envy, like an eating disorder or maybe a secret augmentation surgery. He seethed as he sat and watched.

Treatment or not, Sam was pretty sure Sara hadn't been suddenly cured of her evil streak. Someone like Sara didn't have a conscience at all, so how could she be expected to learn from her mistakes? Beige felt differently. Maybe it was because Beige, along with Ethan, had been friends with Sara since childhood. They loved the old Sara, the one they grew up playing and laughing with. They couldn't believe that she might not be that girl anymore.

But Sam believed. After his talk last year with Sara, there was no way she'd be resuming a friendship with Beige. Even if she wanted to, he'd scared her enough to keep her at a distance. He didn't feel an ounce of guilt about the way he'd played with her fear of his family and their magic. Marisa did, though. She'd told him how it ate away at her that she knew what he'd done and Beige didn't. Everyone else thought it was Marisa's walk and talk with Ethan that had done the trick, but they both knew better.

Marisa wanted Beige kept safe as much as he did, so he trusted her not to talk. He actually took comfort in the fact that Marisa was with Beige every day at school and could keep an eye out for Sara. They had a pact, a pact of protection that, if Beige ever knew about, would royally piss her off.

"Things are normal here."

Disgust lodged in his throat and formed a lump he couldn't swallow. He put the car into gear and headed to Fortunes. With the death of his dad seven years ago, Clairee had come into enough insurance money to start her psychic business. She'd also put back enough to pay college tuition for him and Lilah. Unfortunately, it wasn't enough for him to live on campus so Sam was still living in the family home above the shop. Even with his job at the coffee house, it was a struggle to pay for the extras like his books and student activities fees.

He didn't really mind living at home. He saw Beige more often. She was usually over after school working on her tarot reading with his mom. The privacy issue was challenging because although Beige's parents traveled frequently, her younger brother Charlie, now a freshman at Garrison Prep, was always around. Clairee was pretty cool about giving them space. She didn't mind Beige being in his room and didn't snoop that much. For all he knew, Clairee might already know everything that went on between them, but if she did, she kept it to herself.

He glanced down at his phone and realized it was too late to call Marisa without Beige knowing. He usually checked in with her every other day to see what was happening with Sara at school. She'd probably be with Beige at the shop by now. He would know by her face if everything was cool.

Music blaring on the radio, Sam pondered the thought that he might be a little too protective of the women in his life. Beige would hate the fact that he'd threatened Sara last year, even more than she would hate the fact that he was still keeping track of her now. But he was the man of the family and had been since that fateful day of his father's death. Beige and Marisa were family now, and he'd naturally added them to the list with his mom and Lilah.

He wondered if Marisa knew that. They'd been friends longer than he'd known Beige, but she probably thought he was just working with her to make sure Beige stayed safe. Marisa was a sweet kid that didn't trust herself or her abilities enough yet; how could he not want to take care of her, too. Marisa had no idea of her true beauty or worth. Sam thought about Beige. In his heart no one could compare, but objectively speaking Marisa was the stunner. It was crazy that Ethan hadn't noticed yet how head over heels she was for him.

Sam felt bad about how happy that made him. He still got bad vibes when he was anywhere near Ethan, but he was willing to chalk them up to jealousy of the guy ever having touched Beige. If Ethan could make Marisa happy, give her more confidence or help her see what she meant to the people who loved her, Sam could easily forgive and forget.

A song about how wonderful the world is came on the radio and it kicked him back into positive mode. It had been his dad's favorite tune and when Sam heard it, it was as if he could feel his dad in the car with him. It had always been like that. The song made his heart feel full and he knew that wherever his dad was physically, his soul was always with him.

He was more sure of that than ever now that he had experienced connecting with someone who had crossed over. True, he wasn't a natural at it, like Lilah seemed to be, but he was sure it would happen again. He'd been secretly hoping ever since seeing Keira that his dad would find a way to connect. More than anything, Sam wanted to know what had happened when his dad died. The facts were few and far between. He knew his dad had left home on a regular errand. His mom had received a call, and that call had ended life as he knew it.

It had been a car accident, but Sam's suspicious mind always wrestled with alternate truths. What if it hadn't been an accident at all? His parents hadn't been normal. Garrison was a small and somewhat bigoted town. What if someone had found out what his parents could do, or his dad had crossed a line with his gifts? Anyone could have made it look like a car accident for a price, and there was no lack of money in Garrison despite the small town status.

Sam shook his head, trying to clear the dangerous thoughts from his brain. He couldn't go there; he had people who needed him. He pulled into the driveway behind the house. Since the witch shop was the front, he rarely parked on the street. As he exited the car, he heard the friendly screeches of his little sister Lilah and her new friend Katie. He loved that Lilah was connecting with someone. He only hoped she knew enough to keep her talents under wraps. He doubted fifth grade parents would be excited to have their daughter hanging out with a kid who could speak to the dead.

"What's going on little ladies?" he called to them as he walked towards the back door. Lilah almost tackled him with her hug.

"I miss you, Sam! You're never around anymore!" Wagging her finger at him she continued in a censorious voice, well beyond her years, "I thought you were still living with us!"

Sam let his fingers twirl one of the dark spirals swinging from the back of her head. "I'm here as much as I can be, Lilah. College is hard. You don't want me flunking out, do you?"

"You couldn't flunk out, Sam. You're too smart."

"Thanks for the compliment, kiddo. But it's not always about smarts." He turned to recognize Katie, "What kind of trouble are you two into today?"

The young girl batted her eyes at him as she reported that they were walking up the street for ice cream and invited him along. "Crazy," he thought to himself. He wasn't ready to think of Lilah flirting with boys yet. Maybe she should look for a different friend, but watching them skip off hand in hand, he couldn't help but be happy. It must have been lonely growing up around him and Clairee. He'd been more like a father than a brother. Thinking back, he wasn't sure he'd been good at either role.

He walked into the kitchen and could hear the laughter in the reading room. "The gang's all here," he thought as he pushed the swinging door between the kitchen and the front of the shop quietly so he could observe them without being noticed. He shouldn't have bothered. When he peeked around the corner three sets of female eyes stared right back at him.

"Hola, chicas."

Beige jumped to her feet and laid a big fat kiss right on his lips which had Marisa looking to Clairee with embarrassment. She was always uncomfortable with their public displays of affection. Their feelings for each other were palpable. It was like an electrical current on the air, and she couldn't help thinking she shouldn't be a part of such private things. But they weren't in private, so she cleared her throat before the hello kiss could turn into anything else.

It would have too, despite Clairee's presence. Marisa couldn't believe that Clairee didn't say anything to them. Her own mother would have grounded her until graduation if she had dared to kiss a boy in front of her. Then again, the chances of that actually happening were so slim that given the opportunity Marisa thought she might risk it.

"Well, since you two will probably want some alone time I think I'll be heading out." She stood and walked towards the shop.

"Wait, Marisa." It was Clairee who spoke up. "I have something for you. It came in with a shipment this week, and when I held it I knew it belonged to you." She walked quickly from the room and came back with an object wrapped in rose silk. "Sit, sit. I want to see your face when you open it."

She seated herself next to Marisa and watched anxiously as Marisa folded the silk slowly away from a small silver dagger with a square-shaped emerald below the razor sharp blade.

When Marisa realized what she holding she gasped and raised it reverently just inches from her face. "It's so beautiful, Clairee. I don't...I don't know what to say."

"Thank you will suffice." Getting a little misty she continued, "A beautiful dagger for a beautiful witch. Its vibrational energy matches yours exactly, Marisa. I've never felt anything like it. Can you imagine the circle you can cast with that, my darling?"

Marisa could imagine, and she couldn't wait to get home and try it. She looked at Clairee, wondering what she had done to deserve such a wonderful mentor and friend. "This is the nicest thing someone had ever done for me, Clairee. I mean, I have gotten presents before, but I've never had anyone get me anything that felt so right! It's like you know who I am on the inside."

Marisa said this so incredulously that Clairee laughed out loud before responding, "But Marisa, I do."

Chapter Five

Joy coursed through her veins the entire drive home. She couldn't wait to use the athame in a spell. It was the first gift she'd ever received where she felt like the giver had truly thought about who she was and what she would like. Too many memories of sweaters, purses, earrings, and spa trips filled her mind to the point that she almost missed the turn off onto the curving road that led to her house.

Pulling into the driveway she noticed the darkened windows. "Home Alone" could have been the title of her life if it wasn't already a movie. Her parents were probably studying the same line from the bible they'd studied for the past 3 weeks. How they could spend so many hours on one verse was beyond her. Then again, if she was studying spells she'd have given it her full attention for as long as it took to get it right, so she chalked it up to passion and entered through the side door.

Faced with stairs that led either upstairs or down, she chose up and flicked the light as she entered the kitchen. It smelled like turkey and mashed potatoes. Her mother had left her a plate of food before leaving. The warm feeling from the shop started creeping back. Her mom might have been clueless as to who she really was, but she loved her. In her own special way, in the only way she knew how, she loved her. Marisa considered her life, and in that moment realized she was blessed to have good parents, good friends, and a passion for magic. Of those three, most people were lucky to have one.

"Perfect." She spoke aloud to herself. She knew in an instant the first circle she would cast with the dagger. "A thanksgiving spell of love and protection." She almost held back her shriek of excitement thinking someone would make fun of her, but looking around, she noticed how totally alone she was and let it rip. "And, it's the perfect time to do some magic." She looked at the clock and calculated three hours until her parents would return.

Upstairs in her room, she took out the hidden black boxes and set up her candles in the north, south, east and west positions. Her silver cauldron and herbs sat in the center next to the small chalice with water, a delicate dish filled with salt, and the incense burner that she rarely lit, despite its importance, because it was a dead giveaway to her parents that something out of the ordinary was occurring. Knowing them, they'd probably suspect she was smoking pot before they ever came up with witchcraft. Funny that both would probably still get her in the same hot water.

Marisa unwrapped the rose colored silk and examined the intricate silver carvings in the handle of the dagger. She recognized swirling lines as Celtic knots and felt a flash of familiarity as she gazed at the emerald. Square cut and deep green, it looked valuable. Surely Clairee wouldn't have given away something she could have sold and made a profit from. Looking at the clean iron blade she knew that anyone, whether a witch or not, would have paid an arm and a leg for this athame. Treasure didn't even begin to do it justice.

She held it firmly in her right hand and began the clockwise turning of the circle. As she passed each candle a flame appeared and she called out to the forces of earth, fire, water, and air. She danced in smaller circles inside and allowed the feelings inside her to bubble out in her chant. "Thanksgiving I give, Much love I receive, Protect those that I love and never shall leave." She sat quietly in the center and drew a deep breath as she began to visualize the people she called by name. "By the power of earth protect Lilah and Clairee. By the power of fire be with Beige and Sam, May the power of water help my parents stay safe, and let the power of air keep Ethan whole and unharmed."

When she called upon air to watch over Ethan, a chill ran down her spine and she almost opened her eyes. She felt the athame grow warm in her hand--almost to the point where it was becoming uncomfortably hot--but she stayed with her spell. She wasn't finished. She tried to breathe deeply again, but when the air wouldn't come she began to pant, feeling the room closing in on her. It hadn't been this cold when she'd started the spell. She felt goose bumps rise on her arms. Something wasn't right. If she opened her eyes the spell might not take but she had to open her eyes.

Instead of the expected light and warmth of her room, there was blackness and cold. She didn't know where she was. The sounds of nature led her to believe she was outdoors and she could breathe freely again, so that was something good at least, but she still felt very close to panic. The scent of damp moss filled her nostrils and she heard water rushing in what she thought would be a creek, if she could see. What the hell had happened? She sat perfectly still holding the dagger, now cold like the world that surrounded her. If danger was present it was perhaps her only hope of survival.

As her eyes adjusted, she could see small white caps bursting over randomly scattered solid dark shapes. Her heightened senses didn't seem to be picking up danger, but she couldn't be too careful. A cloud passed from the moon and the bright night light shown through the trees like long ghostly fingers reaching for the forest floor. Beneath the sound of water she could make out another sound more familiar, an even pattern that reminded her of when her grandmother fell asleep in her chair. She looked down to her side and jumped in fright at the figure on the ground beside her.

Marisa's already racing heart felt like it would burst from her chest, but whomever it was appeared to be sleeping soundly, so soundly that the person didn't even flinch at her sudden movement. She noticed the blankets that covered the ground and the remnants of a fire that had long past gone out. The figure next to her stirred and shifted. She thought she could just make out a face. That face then turned and snuggled its way onto her lap.

"Oh my God. What do I do? What do I do? Ohhhhhhhh." For a moment her racing heart was beating for a different reason. She hummed steadily to herself and tried opening and closing her eyes over and over again. She shook her hands the way she always did before totally freaking out, a movement Beige called "jazz hands". Her friend liked to joke that with the sound of the humming Marisa was a one woman Broadway show, but she had no clue why that was so funny.

She closed her eyes tightly again, hoping that when she opened them she'd be back in her room. Slowly opening her left eye, she stole a quick glance at the head of curly dark hair splayed against her thighs. Her mouth formed a black hole of horror.

Ethan? But it wasn't Ethan, It couldn't be Ethan. This wasn't real. She must have fallen asleep during the spell. Maybe she was lucid dreaming, like what happened to Beige last year. But she felt awake, and she could feel the warmth of this stranger's body touching hers, contrasting the icy cold breeze through the trees. If this was a dream, despite the shock and fear, she wasn't so sure she wanted to wake up. In real life what were the odds a boy like this would put his head in her lap?

The young man shifted and raised his head in confusion. His voice was slurred with sleep and difficult to understand.

"Nora…" He pushed his head up off of her lap and looked at her with liquid brown eyes, almost black in the night. "What's wrong? Have they come for you?" His voice gained clarity as fear crept into it.

Marisa looked into his eyes, but didn't know the answer. She opened her mouth to speak but she was dizzy and closed her eyes to fight a wave of nausea. It would be her luck to throw up on the most beautiful person in the world. The nausea increased and disorientation overwhelmed her. She could feel the temperature changing around her body and the athame, again, gaining in heat. She was moving, leaving, but she didn't want to. Not yet. Not until she knew who this Nora was, and why the boy had Ethan's eyes.

She awoke suddenly in her room at home. The candles had gone dark and the clock by her bed showed two hours had passed since she started her protection spell. Two hours? But it had been barely ten minutes. Where had she gone all that time? Physically she was sure she never left her bedroom, but her spirit had traveled someplace else entirely. She was as sure of that as she was that Ethan, or the boy that looked like Ethan, had acted like they were way more than just friends. Impossible. She'd never even been close to being way more than friends with anyone. Ever.

The dagger in her hand was ice cold. Hadn't it been burning hot before? She looked down at her hand and stared in fear at the red marks of a Celtic knot branded into her palm. As if noticing made it real, she felt the pain course through her left hand and up her arm.

"I have to close the spell."

She'd never been hurt before. She'd had close calls with fire and a few poisonous herbs but they had been her fault, not the magic's. "This," she thought, "is different. This is scary, and real, and I want out! Now." She stood, raised the athame, and cut the circle, moving out into the bedroom.

As soon as she was clear of the circle she dropped the dagger and ran to her bathroom. Her mom had given her a burn kit the Christmas before, and she'd thrown it in the bathroom thinking it was a crappy gift.

"Now, not so much." She smeared the aloe over the burn that at closer inspection seemed to be a surface wound. "Still," she thought to herself, "it will probably leave a scar. How do I explain a Celtic knot seared into my hand to my parents?"

She began to carefully clean up her belongings, trying not to hit her burn against the occult supplies. She was lucky no one had come home while she "wasn't there." Better to have been caught actively doing magic, than not in her own body. The more she thought about it, the more astral projection was starting to make the most sense. Her parents would never be able to wrap their minds around that one. She was surprised that she seemed to accept what happened so easily.

Then again, after experiencing a circle where Clairee had channeled the dead, astral projection was child's play. She had somehow managed to leave her body and travel to another place on earth. In that place, there just happened to be someone who looked exactly like Ethan, and when he woke up, he mistook her for a girl named Nora. Mystery solved.

But astral projection wasn't something you stumbled into. She was nowhere near the level witch she would need to be to accomplish something so rare.

Marisa immediately went for her sketch pad and charcoal, the face of the other Ethan flashing again and again in her mind. She wanted to put him and as much of their surroundings as she could on paper so her mind wouldn't embellish the memories with time.

She focused first on the features so familiar to her, his eyes and lips. She was embarrassed to admit she had studied them in detail on the real Ethan when he wasn't looking, roaming his face in her mind like her eyes were a brush on canvas. This new Ethan's hair was longer, and his clothing was strange. He'd worn a plain white shirt with long sleeves, but it wasn't a tee, and the material was stiff and somewhat itchy. Now that she thought of it, the blankets had been different too. If she'd astral projected to another place on this earth, wouldn't they have been in sleeping bags? Seriously, who slept in the middle of the forest in blankets?

He'd spoken to her in English so it obviously wasn't a foreign country...well, not a non-English speaking foreign country anyway. Where did that leave her? And, what was it he had said to her? She had been so startled when he called her Nora that she hadn't heard what came next. He'd sounded scared. Not of her, but of something that could happen to her.

A boy of Ethan's size, and even if he wasn't the real Ethan, he was close enough, would never have been scared by a short redhead like herself. Unless...what if he thought she was a ghost?

That would have frightened him for sure. Marisa could only imagine what she would have thought if she had been rudely awakened in the middle of the night by someone who hadn't been there when she went to sleep.

His words she hadn't been able to remember sprang to her mind. "Have they come for you?" Who had he been talking about? Had who come for her? He hadn't been scared of her, he'd been scared for her. Maybe she had been in real danger.

She heard movement in the house below and quickly scanned the room for errant witchy objects. Satisfied there were none, she slid the sketch pad underneath her pillow and pulled the biology book from the backpack next to her bed, not a moment too soon. Her mother walked into her room without knocking as usual.

"What a night! Are you still up?" She sat on the edge of Marisa's bed still clothed in her maroon cashmere sweater, beige silk slacks and single strand of pearls. Could they be any more different? Her mother was perfect. Always beautiful, always put together, and always knew the right thing to say.

"You have no idea." Marisa yawned and stretched her arms for effect. "I'm almost ready for sleep. A few more minutes, OK?"

Marisa's mom pursed her lips and pretended to think about it. Her eyes went from the open bio book to Marisa, and back again. "Alright, but I want lights out at 10:30, OK?"

"Yes, ma'am." She walked over and gave her mother a hug and kiss. 10:30? What a joke. Marisa did always have her lights out by 10:30, but considering her parents were asleep by 11:00

themselves, she never needed to keep them out for long. Her mom stiffened slightly at first contact but melted at the unexpected sign of affection.

"What was that for, sweetie? I never get kisses goodnight anymore."

Marisa fought back the fear at what she wanted to say. A little voice inside said, "Think of how Beige does it. Just say it out loud. Put your feelings out there. No fear."

She spoke as fast as possible so she wouldn't lose her nerve.

"I love you, Mom. I'm thankful for you. I never say it, but I am." An overwhelming sense of relief flooded through her tense muscles. She did it. It was over and it hadn't hurt at all. She braced a little anticipating possible rejection. They weren't people that said I love you out loud. What if her mom didn't respond?

Her mom's eyes welled up with tears. "I love you too, Marisa." She turned to walk from the room, took one look back over her shoulder, as if to see if what happened had really happened, and closed the door.

Marisa pulled the sketch pad back out.

"I love you too, Ethan…or whoever you are."

Chapter Six

Sam and Lilah sat at their usual table in the local ice cream parlor, each licking a cone full of raspberry chocolate chip. There were other great flavors of course, but in the Reece family you only ever ordered one kind. It was an unspoken gesture of loyalty to their dad who had been on his way to pick some up when he was in the tragic accident that took his life. It seemed like a silly gesture but it felt right to both of them.

"How are things with your new friend, Katie?" Sam asked, almost dropping his cone before he righted it again.

Lilah giggled in the way only a fifth grader could. "You're such a klutz, Sam." She paused and thought about things. "I guess they're fine. I've never had a best friend. I kind of don't know how to act. I don't want to be a creeper, but I really like hanging out with her and want to be around her all the time. Is that OK?"

"Hmmm." He took a few licks before answering, "I think if someone's your true friend they don't care how many things you ask them to do. They want to be around you too. Everyone needs somebody, Lilah, whether it's a best friend or a someone special."

"Like you have Beige?"

He nodded.

"Who does mom have, Sam?" Lilah's face was sad, and Sam could feel his heart sink with sympathy. She felt things so strongly. He didn't doubt she had empathetic abilities along with the psychic ones. He put on his best imitation of a confident big brother smile just in case he could still fool her.

"She's got us, you goofball." He touched the tip of his cone to her tiny nose leaving a pink dot that she wiped off with her sleeve. It must have worked because she smiled and moved onto a new topic of conversation. He would have to think about how to address that later, maybe talk it over with Beige. Lilah was perceptive. She may have been easily distracted in the moment, but if she was starting to worry about their mom and how alone she was without their dad, it would come up again, and next time it wouldn't be so easily put down.

"Sam, do you ever hear voices anymore?"

"You mean since Keira?"

Lilah shook her head while licking her cone. The mixture of gestures seemed to say yes and no at the same time.

"No – I don't. But I'm open to them now. They don't freak me out so much anymore. I'll tell you a secret…"

"What?" She leaned forward and looked deep into his eyes like she was trying to see it.

"I've been trying to see if I can get the voices to talk to me on purpose. I'm hoping that one day I'll be able to talk to Dad."

Lilah's face made a funny little jump. "Of course she'd be curious," Sam thought to himself. Lilah had never really known their father.

Lilah tried hard not to make eye contact as her stomach hit the floor. Did Sam know her secret?

"Does it work?" She kept the conversation totally about Sam. As long as they weren't discussing who she could hear or see (she had discovered she could do both at the Halloween party last year before Beige ended up in the hospital), her secret was safe.

"No, I told you I haven't heard anyone since Keira. But, now that we're talking about this, I think maybe you shouldn't tell Katie about any of your..." he searched for the right word, "...'talents'." He smiled at the thought. She truly was talented, if not in the conventional way.

"Well duh." Lilah went back to licking her ice cream and Sam contemplated how quickly kids went from thinking you were all-knowing to "duh"ing you every other sentence. Lilah hadn't even hit puberty yet; what nightmares would hormones bring? He'd become accustomed to how his thoughts were more like a father's than big brother's and had a moment of sadness at the freedom he'd lost over the years.

Still, looking at Lilah, he wouldn't have it any other way. She was a true gift. She was the one person in the world, even more so than Beige, that he felt all the way comfortable with. He was sure that no matter what, forever and ever, he had Lilah and Lilah had him.

"You can't tell him about me yet."

Lilah jumped at the deep voice and the sight of the man standing right behind Sam. It was like looking at Sam 20 years in the future. The man was heavier and more wrinkly, but he had Sam's kind ocean eyes and wide cheeks. If Sam noticed her shift in attention, he didn't say anything. He had taken his phone out of his pocket and was texting, probably a love note to Beige. Lilah shook her head up and down to let the man know she understood.

He had been visiting her for almost a year now without very much to say. It was always the same. He'd show up, watch them for a while, smile and leave. Every once in a while he would give some weird piece of advice that she usually didn't understand until after whatever it had been about happened. Like when he had told her that gloves were important. The next day while staring at her red chapped fingers after a snowball fight with Sam, she realized he had been trying to help her. She just didn't seem to get him somehow. She didn't understand yet why she couldn't tell her mom or Sam. Didn't he understand how much they both missed him? Didn't he care that her mom was alone?

"I care a lot, Peanut."

She raised her head again at the endearment. Her mom had told her it was his nickname for her. It was different hearing it in his own voice, from his own mouth. She wished she had real memories of him. She quickly dropped her head before Sam could notice.

Sam popped the last of his cone in his mouth, slid his phone in his pocket and stood at the table.

"Ready Freddie?"

The familiar kiddie phrase made her groan.

"Ugh. Why do you always say that?" She looked at her ice cream. "I can't finish this anyway." She scooted past the man no one else could see and dropped the cone in the trash. Grabbing Sam's hand she walked out of the shop.

Chapter Seven

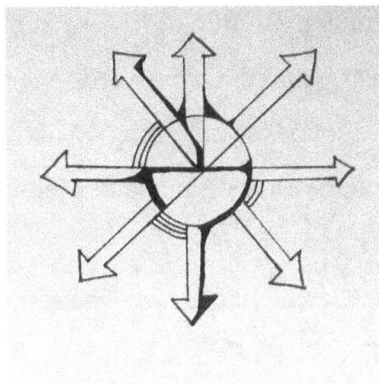

Marisa read the text as she strolled down the hall next to Beige. Surreptitiously she texted, "All Quiet on the Western Front." Sam was one of the few people that enjoyed her literary references, and it was a quick way to let him know all was well with the other witch in their lives. Beige didn't think of herself as a witch, but Marisa did.

There really wasn't a big need to worry. Sara pretty much steered clear of the two of them at school. If their paths did cross, she usually couldn't be bothered to look down her sculpted, and she did really mean sculpted, nose at them. Beige was rambling about a chemistry test that she had obviously bombed.

"I want your help next time, OK? I know you've got to be better at real chemistry than you are with your potions. It's mostly math, and you know you're good at that!"

"Yeah, OK, I can study with you next time. Let me know when the test is."

Beige stopped walking and looked Marisa up and down.

43

"Spill."

"What?" Turning a bright red, Marisa kept walking. Why was she such a bad liar? She should have waited to text Sam back. Now, she was going to have to make something up and pulling one over on Beige was not going to be easy. It made her feel guilty despite her good intentions.

"Marisa, I've been having a conversation with myself since we walked out of English. It's Ethan, isn't it? Something's happened and you don't want to jinx it by telling me. Was the text from him?"

She was caught. Now she would have to bold face lie.

"No, it was Mom. She wants me to go past my grandma's after school to check on her."

"Marisa," Beige rolled her eyes, 'if you're determined to lie to me I think you can do better than that."

The tone of annoyance in Beige's voice wasn't there very often. Marisa knew that if she didn't fess up, and Beige found out the truth, it could get ugly. Still, if Beige knew her best friend and boyfriend were conspiring to keep her safe from Sara without her knowledge, it would get ugly anyway. She thought about the spell and the astral projection. If she told her about that it might distract her, but it would also take them headlong into a conversation Marisa wasn't ready to have.

"Well, if I had any doubt you were keeping something from me, your silence speaks for itself." In one swift move, before Marisa could react, Beige had the cell phone in her hand and was looking through her texts.

Two girls walked right into Beige as she stopped full on in the middle of the crowded hallway. She shrugged them off and flashed a look of anger Marisa had never seen before. Marisa knew that the look wasn't for the girls who had bumped her. Recognition of what she was reading dawned, and bewildered eyes looked from Marisa to the phone and then back to Marisa.

"These aren't from Ethan. They're from Sam."

The hurt, evident in her voice, made Marisa's stomach clench. She felt like she might get sick. "Yes, but they're not what you think…"

"You have no idea what I think, Marisa."

A chill went through her body. She could feel the ice in Beige's voice. She jumped back and fumbled to catch the small purple cell hurled with venomous force in her direction. She looked up to try to explain, but Beige's back was already down the hallway. Tears tumbled over the edge of her amber lashes while she tried very hard to keep the sob wedged deep in her throat from escaping. Looking around, she had nowhere to go. She was surrounded by people. Curious eyes watched her every move. To her right, a red door caught her attention and she ducked into the janitor's closet to wait for the bell to ring and the hall to clear.

Once inside the darkness, safe in a cocoon of brooms and cleaning fluids, she let the tears flow. So that was what a fight felt like. She had never experienced this particular rite of friendship, not with anyone that mattered. An only child with perfect parents and no real friends never had anything to fight about. Beige was her first best friend, her only genuine friend.

It wasn't like it was really that bad, right? She'd been trying to protect her. Her heart had been in the right place. Beige had to be able to see that in time, but it didn't feel like she would. Instead of the relief she thought they would bring, the tears seemed to bring on a tightening like a fist around her heart and her lungs couldn't draw in enough breath to push the pain out.

What if Beige couldn't forgive her? What if she had truly lost her best friend? Marisa dropped her books and leaned back against a wall, knocking over a mop shoved into a bucket. The large crash must have sounded in the hall because the sudden glare of fluorescent lighting pierced the darkness. The panic she was starting to feel doubled in intensity when she heard a familiar voice say her name. She turned but there was no other way out. Hiding her hands in her face she tried to sound as normal as possible.

"I'm fine, Ethan. You can go to class, really."

How embarrassing could this get? He had to know she was crying; there was no way he could miss the sniffles in between the words. Her internal voice begged with such ferocity that she almost moved her lips, "Please, God. Please let him turn around and leave."

The door shut and blackness enveloped them both. A hand touched her shoulder. It was warm and she jumped with surprise. The hand pulled and turned her into arms that smelled like woods and rushing water. For a moment she stayed stiff, afraid to move and have the moment disappear like the one in her spell. But this wasn't her spell, it was the reality of the janitor's closet, and she was in Ethan's arms. She felt her body go limp, unable to deny herself the comfort her broken heart sought.

He didn't say anything, just held her. She felt his hand on the back of her head. He stroked her carrot colored waves as she pressed her face against the hard muscles of his chest. The tightness in her lungs was replaced with a deep tugging, a longing to be held, and understood. In the silence, her breathing steadied and she thought she felt his quicken. She was instantly and acutely aware of his hand on her waist. His chin rested against the top of her head and he shifted so that the hand on her waist dropped to hold hers, letting their fingers intertwine.

They stood like that for what seemed like forever. With each passing second Marisa wished fervently for it all to last just a little bit longer. With his free hand he tipped her chin skyward and for one beautiful second she thought he might kiss her, but he only wiped the tears from her cheeks. She lowered her lashes wondering how a person could go from the depths of despair to the heights of ecstasy, then back to the depths of despair in mere moments.

As she opened her mouth to speak the bright lights interrupted her train of thought. Before her eyes could adjust he was gone, out the door, without a word. Gone, and the moment was over. The breath she didn't know she'd been holding rushed out in one sharp exhalation. She bent over and picked up her books, peeking her head around the corner in time to see Ethan's chocolate curls disappear into Mrs. Rammer's English room. Marisa squared her shoulders, straightened her sweater, and started towards the lab.

She reached up to wipe her eyes in an attempt to remove any streaks of wayward eye make-up and stopped mid-motion. She slowly turned her hand palm side up. Tingles traveled up her spine. The pink skin of her hand looked new and soft. She glanced at her other hand to make sure there was no mistake. The dark red lines of the burns etched into her hand during the end of her spell were nowhere to be seen. It was like they'd never existed. But they had been there before. She had seen them when she was texting Sam. They had been hurting right before her fight with Beige.

Marisa physically recalled the memory of Ethan's body holding hers. There had been a moment where he had held her hand in his. It almost escaped her memory because she had been thinking of a kiss, but it had happened, she was sure. What strange magic had she created in the closet? Was it possible to heal herself without effort or knowledge? Or had Ethan played a role? Impossible. She would have to talk with Clairee.

Chapter Eight

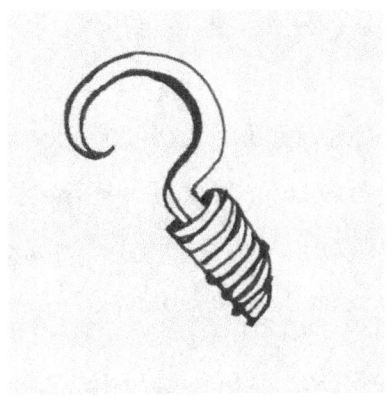

Sam looked at the clock on the wall as his biology professor continued his lecture on Mendel. He twirled his pencil, counted the number of steps in the lecture hall, and wondered if the girl in the opposite row knew that she had a muffin top.

He didn't understand why a police officer needed biology. Anatomy and physiology, first aid, crime scene investigation techniques, those all made sense, but biology? He couldn't think of any circumstance where he would need to understand recessive genes.

Blond hair was from a recessive gene. So was red. His thoughts turned to Marisa and he wondered if she and Beige would be at the shop when he finished class. He'd tried texting her at the end of the day but she hadn't responded and he didn't want to be late for bio class.

The lecture ended and the professor assigned some light reading over the weekend while reminding them of an upcoming test on Tuesday. Sam gathered his belongings and walked out to the car.

It was colder than he'd expected and he scanned the backseat for his sweatshirt. Instead his eyes rested upon the card Beige had given him last week sticking out of his backpack. He couldn't resist picking it up and reading the words again. "To my true love and hero - Thank you for teaching me to open up. Thank you for showing me someone could love me just as I am. And, thank you for showing me there is someone in the world that deserves 100% of my trust. Forever yours, Beige."

He was one lucky man. No doubt about that. Maybe he should stop off and get her some flowers to surprise her. They would add color to her grey day, like she added color to his life. Tuning the radio to his favorite alternative station, he noticed it was close to four o'clock. The flowers would have to wait for another day. He found himself singing out loud and smiling as he pulled into the lot behind the house, but his smile faded as he realized that the only other car there belonged to Clairee.

Still, that didn't mean Beige wasn't around. She could have walked from the coffee shop or had Marisa drop her off. He opened the door, stepped into the kitchen and was immediately accosted by Lilah.

"How could you, Sam! You're such a jerk." She shoved him, actually shoved him, and he fell back into a chair, dropping his backpack to the side.

"Whoa there, lady, what's with the violence? Doesn't a guy get a fair trial before you convict him in this house?"

"Not when you mess things up with the best thing in our life, Sam." She turned her back to him and crossed her arms. He reached for her shoulder and gently tugged her back towards him.

"Come here, you. Let's talk about this. What did I do?"

"I don't know, Sam, but I know that whatever you did she's thinking that it's over. I can feel how angry she is with you. She's not coming back to this house. You've ruined everything."

A wave of fear passed through Sam's body and he felt like he was going to get sick. His face went white and his voice deserted him as he opened his mouth, but nothing came out. Lilah gave him one more angry look before she turned and ran from the room.

"Shit."

What had he done? Even as he asked himself the question, he knew. There was only one thing that could make Beige stop talking to him, besides cheating, which he would never in a million years even think about. He'd been absolutely faithful.

"Shit, shit, shit," he swore again as he stood up to go find his mom. Clairee sat quietly in the parlor, turning over cards, obviously deep in thought. He looked down and saw the Devil. He prayed to God that the reading she was doing wasn't for him and Beige.

"Sit down, Sam." Matter of fact, not even looking up, she had to be angry too.

"Mom, I didn't know she'd find out, we were just trying to protect her." As he heard his own words, for the first time he thought of Marisa. "Double shit."

"Don't curse in my parlor, Sam." She flipped another card. The Hanged Man stared back at him, swinging lamely from a rope around the ankle.

Sam had known from the moment Lilah implied Beige was angry that it was about them protecting her from Sara, but he had forgotten that if Beige knew what was going on, he wasn't the only one who would be facing her wrath.

"Well, things do not look good, Mr. 'Big strong man who has to protect his poor little woman from the evil cheerleader'. I've done this reading every which way I can think of and your cards are abysmal. What were you thinking?" She sat the deck down and looked directly into Sam's eyes.

"I wasn't, Mom. I went with my gut. Sara's evil, we know that! Beige had to be protected. She thinks that Sara can be reformed, that there's still good in her, but Marisa and I both know there's not. She hurt her once and she'd do it again in a heartbeat. If I hadn't confronted her last year…"

"You what?" Clairee gasped. "Sam! I knew you were lying to protect her, but you're saying you confronted Sara last year and never told us? How could you do that? After everything we went through together. Our lives were in each other's hands and you were keeping something back? That could have put us all in extreme danger. I would never have done the channeling if I'd known our group wasn't whole."

"No, Mom, I wouldn't have let that happen. I confronted Sara after the channeling, while Marisa was talking with Ethan. I couldn't help it. The cards that night ended with justice. I didn't believe justice could happen without confrontation. She had to be scared. She had to know there would be consequences if she went after Beige again. And she hasn't, has she? Beige has been safe because Marisa and I have done everything possible to make it so."

Madame Clairee placed her hand to her forehead, looking down at the cards and the reversed Star. "Of course, Marisa was involved as well. That makes much more sense." She looked from the cards to Sam's eyes. "Are you an idiot?"

Sam stared at her, not knowing how to react.

"I thought I raised you right. After your father died, I was scared and alone, but I took pride in the fact that I had raised a man who was loving and honest, Sam! Honest! There is nothing more important in a relationship than honesty, and now you and Marisa have not only jeopardized your relationships with the most important person in your lives, you have jeopardized the future of this family."

Sam sunk to the sofa, Clairee's words like a puzzle missing pieces. "What are you talking about, Mom? How could Beige being angry with me risk our whole family? You're overreacting."

"Am I, Sam? Look at these cards. This reading's not about YOU. This reading's about US! Did you forget that Beige is more than the love of your life? She has a destiny and it's my job…all of our jobs to make sure she can fulfill it. You and Marisa have created a breach I'm not sure we can fix. It may seem like a tiny white lie to you, but Beige trusted you with all her heart. She loved you both. She probably thinks I knew about this too, and Lilah!"

"What destiny are you talking about, Mom? You've gone on and on about Beige and the cards and her destiny since the first day I found her in the shop. But you've never been clear! What is she supposed to do? Why is she so damn important to us?"

"Beige plays an integral role in a bigger plan, Sam, one that your father and I set in motion right before he died. Everything we were working towards is now at risk and it's your fault, yours and Marisa's. Congratulations! You protected Beige from Sara! Very good work. Now try and protect us from what's coming next, Sam, if you can."

Clairee threw the cards across the room and stormed up the stairs to the private part of the house where the family kept their rooms. Sam stood and began to collect the cards from the floor. He reached for the Heirophant. Major Arcana card five. Shock waves ran up his arm into his shoulder and he cried out with pain. He dropped the card to the floor, and as he did he saw fire and smelled burning flesh. The face of a man that looked like some kind of Bishop seemed to scowl in judgment and condemnation.

It was over as quickly as it began. Sam picked the card back up and turned it over in his hand. It was just an ordinary tarot card. There seemed to be nothing special about it now. He rubbed his shoulder with his hand and took a deep breath to clear the remembrance of the horrific smell. What had happened and what did it have to do with what his mother had been saying? Clairee had never, in his whole life, spoken to him like that. When she was angry there was always a smile waiting beneath the surface. There had been no smile today. She had been deadly serious and Sam was worried not only for his relationship with Beige, but for the very survival of them all.

Chapter Nine

Lilah sat behind the counter in the shop listening to the screaming in the parlor. She had never heard her mother this angry. Lilah was mad at Sam too, but only because she loved Beige. The idea that Sam had screwed up their destinies and put everyone in danger frightened her. Was that what the strange sinking feeling in her stomach had been about? She watched her mother storm out of the parlor and up the stairs to their rooms. Sam was still inside. Should she go on and talk with him? Could they figure out a way to make it better together? She was about to go to him when she felt a presence at her side.

"It'll all be OK, Peanut. Your mom can't see what's coming and it scares her. She's used to knowing what to expect. You and I know better. Everything is as it should be."

"How can you say that?" Lilah whispered angrily, afraid Sam might hear her talking from the other room.

The man that sat next to her looked down at her with loving eyes. Sam's loving eyes. They looked so much alike.

"You heard what your mother said, Lilah. She and I were involved with something important before I died. Something that would have changed all of our lives for the better. She knows there's still a way to fix it and that Beige is the key, but she's not sure how to do it and she thinks that if Beige isn't here with her, it will be impossible."

"Well, she's right, isn't she?"

"No, there's another way. I found it the morning I died."

"What is it?" she asked.

"If I could remember, Lilah, I would have told you the first time you saw me. I only know how to push people in the right direction. It's just a feeling inside me that compels me to act."

Lilah jumped at the sound of Sam's wince of pain in the parlor.

The man looked towards the parlor and she thought she saw a flash of concern in his eyes. "Don't worry about him, he's fine. I sent him a small vision to guide him."

"And it hurt him?" Lilah asked mouth gaped wide in shock. "You hurt him! You're not good. I don't know who you are, but there's no way you're my dad." She crossed her arms and closed her eyes, wishing him away.

"OK," he gave a quick laugh, "I'm going. But I am your father, Lilah, and I do want what's best for all of you. Promise."

When she opened her eyes, she was alone. Sam walked out of the parlor and straight into the kitchen, not even noticing her. What was with everyone today? Why was everyone so angry? Had Sam really messed everything up as Clairee thought, or was the stranger who claimed to be her father the one who was right? Would it all end up being OK?

Lilah pulled the phone from the counter to where she sat. If no one in her family would talk to her, she'd find someone who would. She'd go to Katie's house where everything was normal and no one got mad. When no one answered she decided that eleven years old was old enough to walk to a friend's by herself.

About six blocks later she realized Katie's house was farther away than she thought and it was starting to get dark. She picked up her pace and kept moving forward, hoping that any minute the right street would appear. The wind whipped her ponytail back and forth as she shifted her bag from one shoulder to the other. It hadn't seemed this heavy at home. One unknown street turned into the next, and Lilah finally gave up.

For one second she felt what she thought was a tear begin to form in her right eye, but she quickly looked skyward and sent it back where it belonged. Lilah Reece didn't cry. Lilah Reece could do anything she wanted, and Lilah Reece did not get lost. She reassessed her situation. The street actually looked a little familiar. She was sure she'd been there before, but it wasn't Katie's street, she was sure of that.

Just as she was about to stand and start walking again, a familiar maroon station wagon pulled to the side of the road. As the window slowly lowered Lilah gave a sigh of relief at the sight of tiger orange curls. Across from the driver sat an elderly woman with hair so white it almost looked blue. Mrs. Goodman and Marisa. She was saved.

"Lilah Reece!" Marisa exclaimed, "What are you doing this far from your house by yourself when it's almost dark?"

"I was walking to Katie's but I think I took a wrong turn. Is there any way you could give me a ride?" Lilah hoped Marisa wouldn't make her go back home. It was the last place she wanted to be.

Mrs. Goodman spoke first. "Get in the car, young lady. We would be happy to take you where you're going. However, I'd first like to know if Madame Clairee knows you're out and about on your own?"

Lilah had forgotten Mrs. Goodman was close to her mother. Of course she would call her when she got home. Lilah had hoped her mom was so angry with Sam that she wouldn't notice her absence for a few hours. If Mrs. Goodman called the shop, she'd be busted for sure.

"She knows." Lilah fibbed. "I was about to call her and tell her I was lost when you pulled up, but if you could get me a ride I wouldn't have to tell her. Please? She'd be upset if she thought I got lost, and she's already upset from an argument with Sam. Please don't make her day worse."

At the mention of the argument with Sam, she noticed a strange look pass from grandmother to granddaughter. Truth be told though, Lilah didn't care. She just wanted to get to Katie's and forget her whole afternoon. As luck would have it, the women seemed to believe her and neither said anything more as she hopped into the backseat and buckled herself in. They drove in relative silence as Marisa turned the car around and headed the other direction. As house after house passed by, Lilah realized she needed to pay more attention when her mom and Sam drove her places. She had been pretty far from Katie's.

As they pulled into the driveway Lilah thought she heard Marisa let out a weird, little breath and wondered if the silver SUV that had pulled in behind them had anything to do with it. She didn't wait to find out. The front door to Katie's was wide open like normal and warm yellow light spilled out onto the porch. "See you later, Marisa. Bye, Mrs. Goodman." She ran as fast as she could inside the house.

Marisa sat very still in the driver's seat. Unsure of what to do next she looked at her grandmother for help. Emma smiled and looked confused. She had no idea what was about to happen. Looking in her side view mirror Marisa watched as the lanky, yet incredibly sexy, Ethan Martos approached the car. He was blocking her in and she had nowhere to go. Only six hours ago, he had left her standing in a janitor's closet in shock and confusion and now here he was again, walking oh so cool and laid back to her driver side window.

He knocked on the glass, a shy smile slowly spreading across his face. "Smiling is good. Smiling is good," she repeated to herself as she stared.

"Yes it is, Marisa, but talking is better." It was her grandmother that brought her back to reality. "Are you going to roll down the window or just stare?" Her grandmother flashed Ethan a toothy smile and elbowed Marisa into action. Marisa hoped not too many seconds had passed. She hit the button that slid the window down and Ethan leaned in over the edge. She instinctively jumped back and he smiled wider.

"Hey, Marisa," his velvety voice almost put her in a trance. What was he doing here and why didn't he stay in his car and let her out?

"Hello, Sir!" Grandma Emma with the save reached out in greeting. "I'm Emma Goodman, this lovely girl's grandmother, if you can believe it." Mrs. Goodman touched her snowy hair as if primping in a mirror and Ethan gave a laugh that sounded almost genuine.

"It's very nice to meet you, Ms. Emma. I'm Ethan. I'm in some of Marisa's classes at Garrison Prep." He turned his attention to Marisa, "I just wanted to check on you. See if you were feeling better than you did at school today?" His eyes shifted, not knowing if her grandmother had any idea of the day's events.

"It's alright, Ethan. Grandma knows everything." Maybe a little too much, she thought as she watched her grandmother's gaze going back and forth between the two.

"Oh, OK then," he paused," I was a few people behind you in the hall when you and Beige got into it. I saw her throw the phone at you. And then..." his voice drifted off. Marisa was pretty sure they were both remembering the janitor's closet. The feel of his arms around her and his smell that she couldn't inhale enough came rushing back. His hand on her hand and the way he had tipped up her chin had overwhelmed her. Did he remember it like she did, or had it all been a mistake to him?

"Yes," she broke the silence, "thank you so much for comforting me. It was the first time I've been in a fight with a friend and I totally didn't know how to react. Everyone was looking at us. You," she looked up into his darkening eyes, "you helped me a lot." He held her gaze for a moment before a slight cough from Ms. Emma reminded them there was another person in the car.

"Well," he replied looking to the passenger seat, "I'll let you get going. I'm blocking you in, but I needed to check on you." He touched her shoulder with his hand and she could feel the turbulence rising in her stomach. It felt more like waves than butterflies. He turned and walked back to his car. As he did both she and her grandmother watched.

"That is one fine looking boy that has his eye on you, sweetie."

'What?" Marisa gave a laugh of embarrassment. "His eye on me? No – he was looking out for me. Really, if you had been there, it was so humiliating. I was a mess, a big blubbering mess."

"Eighty years gives you wisdom enough to know when a boy looks at a girl like that, he's got it bad. He likes you, Marisa."

Marisa backed out of the driveway careful not to look in Ethan's direction. Her grandmother stayed quiet the rest of the trip, leaving her to ponder that very possibility. Did Ethan Martos really like her too?

Chapter Ten

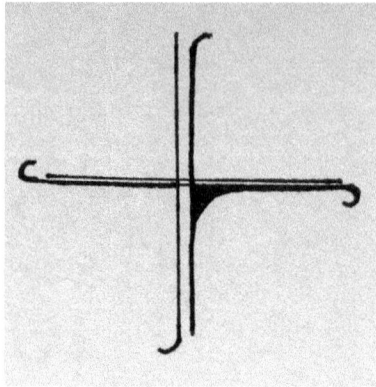

Sam sat in the car outside of Beige's house feeling eerily similar to how he felt the year before, when he had followed her on that fateful date with Ethan. That night he had been unsure as to what danger they might be facing. Tonight he was only worried about himself. He had no doubt she was angry. Beige hadn't returned his calls or texts and she hadn't shown up at Fortunes after school. If she was really not talking to him he wasn't sure what good it would do to be at her house. Charlie, her overprotective little brother, or her parents would help keep him away if that's what she wanted.

Putting the fear and the negativity out of his mind, he got out of the car and made his way to the front door. He felt like a scared kid at a haunted house, not sure he if he wanted her to open up or not. If she didn't open the door, he didn't have to deal with the fact that he'd messed up. It put the conflict off for another day. If she did open the door there was no going back and they would either get through it or not.

Why did relationships have to be so complicated? On second thought, why did he even get into one in the first place? He stopped himself before going down that road. He knew why he was in a relationship. The moment Beige walked into Fortunes last October, he'd been hers. From the initial annoyance at her crush on Ethan, to the intimate sharing of the loss of her aunt and his father, every moment had deepened his belief they were made for each other. Clairee even agreed, telling him they had been together before.

Past lives weren't something he really believed in, but the thought that their souls might be connected by more than what he remembered gave him hope that this was just a bump in the road. Beige was stubborn, he knew that. She would come around. He had good reasons for not telling her about confronting Sara last year. He and Marisa had watched Sara for Beige's own good. Eventually she'd get that.

Almost convinced things would work out for the best, he knocked harder; still no answer. Walking towards the garage, he peeked in and found it empty. If Beige was home she was probably alone and ignoring him on purpose so he ran to the back of the house where the spare key was hidden in the birdhouse Beige had made in third grade.

He flicked the light switch to his right as he entered through the kitchen, scowling momentarily as his eyes adjusted. The Parker kitchen shined spotless. Mrs. Parker never left a mess. Beige, on the other hand, took after her father. He chuckled as he pictured her closet floor two feet deep with clothing. He recalled being enveloped in the smell of her when she had shoved him inside to hide him from her parents who had returned home earlier than expected.

"Beige!" he yelled, deciding the best course of action would be to let her know he was in the house. Visions of a baseball bat to the head flooded his mind and he hoped they weren't premonitions. "Beige!" Like the knock at the door, he was being ignored, if she was there at all. A light in her room didn't necessarily mean she was in the house. Up the stairs, past the family portraits, he walked cautiously to her room, wondering what would happen if her parents came home and found them alone.

When he pushed open her bedroom door he breathed a sigh of relief to see her lying motionless on the bed. He stopped and watched for the steady rise and fall of her chest. As softly as possible, to avoid waking her, he sat on the side of her bed. She let out an unintelligible mumble and rubbed her nose with her hand. He reached out and stroked a strand of her chestnut hair from her cheek. Her eyes flickered open and filled with warmth and surprise, then quickly clouded over.

"What are you doing here?" Her voice was flat and cold.

"I thought we should talk?"

"Seems to me like you've already done enough talking. To Sara. To Marisa. Anyone else you've been talking to that you want to tell me about, Sam?"

"I know you're mad..."

"Oh, I'm not mad. I'm beyond mad. I trusted you, Sam. You knew how I felt about what Sara did. You knew how I wanted the situation handled, but instead you handled me, and I am not a girl that needs or wants handling."

"I know, I'm sorry," he said

"I trusted you."

He thought of the card. "100%," he said quietly.

"Yes." She paused. "Sam, I love you. I was ready to trust you with everything. Every part of myself - body and soul, but now...I don't know. If you could lie to me about something like this, for as long as you did, what else could you keep from me?"

"Nothing, Beige! I would never lie to you."

"You already did."

"That wasn't lying...you never asked if I talked with Sara."

"You knew what I believed, and you let me go on believing it," she said.

"But..." He ran his hands through his dark wavy hair. "I know. I'm sorry."

"I understand that you're sorry you got caught, Sam, but I don't believe you're sorry about what you did. There are two issues of trust going on here. You lied, yes, but you didn't trust me either. You didn't trust me to know what was best for myself. I don't need another parent."

"Beige, you have no idea how evil Sara really is," he pleaded.

"And you have no idea how much good was ever in her or how much is left."

"So, what? You can't forgive me because I don't believe Sara's got good in her? Please, Beige, can't we just get past this?"

"It's not that easy. I'd like you to get out of my house, Sam. For right now we are not together. I don't know if I can be together with you again. Tell your mom I'll call her. I won't be past the shop for a while."

She held her bedroom door open for him.

"Beige, It's important to me that you don't hold this against my mom or Lilah. They knew nothing, and Marisa didn't..."

She cut him off. "Don't even go there, Sam. What happens between Marisa and me is none of your business. I'll deal with her."

"She loves you. You're her best friend," he said.

"And she was mine."

"Was?"

"Friends have to be able to trust, Sam." She looked towards the hall. "Now do I have to see you out?"

Sam stepped from the room, turning back to face her. "We're not over, Beige. You can't decide to end us on your own. I still love you and you still love me."

"Love isn't the issue, Sam, it's trust."

He looked at her one more time, studying her face, like he was memorizing it before he closed her bedroom door and walked slowly down the stairs.

Beige listened for the front door to close and pulled the hidden box of from below her bed. For the past year whenever she was upset, she'd turned to the tarot. She'd found the cards to be a form of therapy, a way for her mind to make sense of the non-magical world around her. She took a deep breath and channeled the pain she felt at Sam and Marisa's betrayal into the reading. What would happen to the three of them? She lit her candle, shuffled the cards and cut them three times. She sifted through the painful images of their faces in her memories. In only one year they had become her whole life. They were all so connected that the lies made her feel as if she'd lost a part of herself. She began laying the cards out in a Celtic cross formation. As she put the last card in the spread there was a knock at the door.

"Sam..." she said under her breath and her heart pounded harder.

The knock sounded again. She didn't want to talk with him anymore, and especially not in the middle of a reading. But she knew him, he'd never give up if he thought it was important. She left her cards and ran downstairs preparing to be kind, but firm. He had to know she wasn't changing her mind.

When she opened the door she was surprised to see Clairee.

"Beige, I'm so sorry. May I come in?"

She was torn. On the one hand she loved Clairee like a mother and wanted to fall into her comforting arms and cry. On the other, Clairee was the mother of the boy she was angry with and trying very hard not to think about. Love and need won, and she waved her arm to welcome Clairee into her home.

"You've never been here before."

"No, not inside. Only out front last year when Sam drove you home."

"Sam." Beige let his name hang in the air between them.

"Listen Beige, as much as I love my son, I'm not here to talk about him...well, not specifically. I need to talk with you about a reading I just finished." She was wringing her hands and swaying from side to side. "And about your destiny."

As strange as it sounded, Beige had come to terms with the reality that she did have a destiny and that Madame Clairee was probably holding back what she really knew about Beige's future. She'd trusted that if she needed to know, Clairee would tell her. Now, when she couldn't be a part of Fortunes or Sam's life any longer, Sam's mother seemed poised to spill her secrets.

"I was doing a reading, too. Upstairs, about Sam and Marisa. Why don't you come up and help me finish and then we can talk. I could use someone to talk with if you can try to be my friend and not Sam's mom.'

"Oh, Beige." Clairee reached out and touched her shoulder, "I've always been and always will be both."

"OK, come on up." She led the way up the same stairs that she had taken Sam the year before. Totally different situation she told herself. Last year, I was in danger. This year he's still overreacting about it all. She opened the door to her room and invited Clairee to sit by the spread and candle on her floor.

"What were you asking?" Clairee's eyes roamed the cards Beige had dealt, widening by the second.

"I was thinking of Sam, Marisa, and myself. Wondering what would happen with us. You can see the Death card in the immediate future. I'm sure it's the end of at least one of those friendships."

"You're wrong." Clairee whispered.

"I know you love all three of us and I know you want us to be able to fix this, but I'm not sure it's possible."

"No, Beige." Tears welled in her eyes. "This time the Death card isn't figurative. Sam's going to die."

Chapter Eleven

Lilah peeked around the corner to see into the parlor room of Fortunes. She took in the uncomfortable scene before hiding behind the counter where she would be able to hear what was revealed in this meeting they hadn't invited her to.

Clairee paced back and forth. It was obvious, even to an eleven year-old, that no one wanted to talk. She knew Sam had given up trying to get Beige to talk with him, and Beige had made it clear she had nothing to say to Sam or Marisa. Marisa couldn't look at Beige without crying, and Lilah could feel that if Marisa and Sam started talking, Beige would get even more annoyed.

The figure beside her spoke, "It's pretty tense in there, huh, Peanut?"

"Go away."

"You're going to want me here soon. They may even want me in there.'

Lilah's eyes widened.

"You have a part in this, Peanut. Let's just listen together. What do you say?"

"OK." she leaned her head back, closed her eyes and focused in on the voices.

Clairee broke the silence. "I'm not sure where to begin."

"It's OK, Mom. Marisa and I still aren't sure why you brought us here, but if it's to try and make us all friends again, or get Beige and I back together, I'm not sure Beige is ready yet."

Beige spoke, "I'm definitely not ready yet, but since I called the meeting along with your mother, I think we can safely assume that's not it, Sherlock."

Lilah wished she could see Sam's face. She loved her brother but she also loved when Beige got sassy with him. Her mom always said Sam could dish it out, but couldn't take it.

"Beige, please. I understand your anger but given what your reading revealed, I think you know this is an extremely serious situation," said Clairee.

"I'm not 100% sure your interpretation was correct," Beige said. "I laid out the cards and asked the question. I think what I saw made more sense."

"There's too much you don't know, Beige. Too much that none of you are aware of. It's time. I just thought...I don't know what I thought. Maybe that it would be clearer."

"Clearer would help me, Mom. Seriously, can you get to the point?"

"What I have to tell you started before any of us were born. It goes back generations...to the founding of Garrison."

"1877," Marisa said to no one in particular.

"Is this connected to my destiny?" Beige asked.

"It's connected to everything. Your destiny, Sam's life, my husband's death."

"It's connected to Dad?"

Lilah heard the fear in Sam's voice and wanted to go to him, but her father put his finger to his lips and shook his head. She closed her eyes again and focused.

Clairee continued, "The town was founded by three families. Descendants of these families all still live here today..."

"The Reece family, the Smith family, and the Lowell family," Marisa interrupted.

"How do you know this shit?" Sam asked.

Marisa answered in a voice Lilah almost couldn't hear, "When we moved here I didn't have friends, Sam. I went to the library a lot. There's a whole section on Garrison's history. I didn't have anything else to do."

Clairee jumped in, "That's right, Marisa. If you follow those families to present day we know that Sam and Lilah are from my husband's family, and Sara's last name is Smith."

"But, I don't know any Lowells," Sam said.

"You actually do," Clairee continued. "Melissa Martos' maiden name is Lowell. Other than her son, she's the last surviving Lowell."

Marisa gasped, "Ethan..."

"Yes," Clairee said. "Ethan. Now, theses three families weren't the only people living in the area."

"The curse," Marisa said. "But, the books said it was only a legend."

"Is your witchcraft a legend, Marisa? There are many very real things that our world closes its eyes to," Clairee answered.

"What's the curse, Marisa?"

This voice surprised Lilah. She didn't think Beige would speak to Marisa at all. It must have surprised Marisa, too because there was a short silence before she answered. Lilah was tired of not being able to watch so she scooted stealthily across the floor towards the door. No one cared about anything outside of the room anyway. Clairee and Beige sat on opposite ends of the couch with Marisa on pillows on the floor. Sam leaned against a wall. She watched as her father's spirit walked into the parlor and sat beside Clairee. Lilah saw her mother take a deep breath and quickly look around, but she knew her mom couldn't see him.

"There were the three families: the Smiths, Lowells, and Reeces, but there was a fourth family that the others shunned. They were French and didn't speak much English. It seemed like every time something bad happened, whether it was drought, disease, attacks on animals by predators...those were all things that happened back in those days," she explained. "Whatever happened, the Denoncourt family was never affected. Their crops survived, their children lived, their animals were protected. It didn't take much for the founding families to believe witchcraft was involved."

"Was it?" Sam looked at Clairee.

"Why ask me, Sam?"

"I think you know," he replied.

"So what does this all have to do with us? How is my destiny connected to these families, Clairee?" Beige asked.

"The Denoncourt family's oldest daughter was named Benedicte. She was beautiful and smart, and the sons from all three of the founding families wanted her, but the families wouldn't consider their marriage to her because of the family's connection to magic. One morning," Clairee continued, "her body was found naked in the creekbed. She'd been beaten and raped. She was seventeen years old."

"Oh my God," Beige said.

"The curse was placed upon the three founding families by the matriarch of the Denoncourt family, Genevieve," Marisa said. "Every 17 years since Benedicte's death a member of one of the founding families has died in some tragic scenario."

"So, my father?" Sam asked.

Clairee looked at Beige. Understanding dawned. "No! It's just a story," Beige screamed. "It's not true. It can't be."

Lilah watched as Beige started trembling and it looked like she couldn't catch her breath. Sam noticed as well. He went to her, pulled her into his arms and asked, "What's the matter? Why is this so bad? It'll be OK, Beige. We have a few more years to figure out what to do. Right, Mom?"

Clairee looked at Sam, and Lilah immediately knew why Beige was upset. She looked to her father and he nodded his head yes.

"Ethan Martos' aunt was killed in a boating accident seventeen years ago this October 31st, Sam."

"But Dad..."

"Your father's death was not connected to the curse, baby, but yours will be."

Beige began sobbing in Sam's arms.

"Beige, I'm not going to die." Sam said.

Marisa watched him shake her by the shoulders to try and get her to calm down.

"Listen to me. Look in my eyes. I'm not going to die." He spoke slowly.

Clairee interrupted, "No, you're not Sam. Your father and I worked too hard and too long to prevent it. The future can be changed. We know that. Nothing is ever set in stone."

Sam stood and walked towards his mother.

"So you're saying this is all true? That both Lilah and I are in danger?"

"Not Lilah. With some help, your father and I were able to foresee that you would be the sacrifice, that's what we were working so hard at before his death. When he left that day, he told me he'd found the way to not only save you, but to put an end to the curse.

The last thing he said to me was that it all had to do with the cards. I assumed he meant the tarot, I've never been able to know for sure."

Beige, who had mellowed somewhat, spoke, "So my destiny, the tarot...do you think all this has something to do with me? Can I save Sam?"

Clairee dropped to the couch, fingers deep in her dark black curls, massaging her skull like she did with her migraines. She rubbed her eyes as if to clear them and looked to Beige.

"I don't know. I think so. The day you came to us I knew you were special. When you started reading the cards without any background or practice I hoped you were somehow connected to what Rafe knew. There's so much you and Sam share. You know I've said you've been together before."

"I don't want to go there, Mom. Beige isn't comfortable with the concept of past lives."

"Past lives?" Marisa chimed in. Something clicked in her head. "I need to tell you all about something that happened to me."

"Not now, Ris, we need to focus on how the cards and my destiny can be used to save Sam."

Lilah watched Marisa's face fall at the annoyance she heard in Beige's voice. She quietly stood and tiptoed to the stairs. She didn't want to watch anymore.

"It will all be OK, baby, I promise," her dad said from behind her.

"Why can't you just tell me what you know? If you tell me, I can tell them, and we can make sure Sam is safe."

"I can't remember, Lilah. That's the God's honest truth."

Chapter Twelve

Marisa smudged the charcoal line with her thumb and grabbed her gummy eraser to sharpen the edge on the glass orb Mrs. Whelan had placed in a still life on the central art room table. She focused intently on getting the reflections exactly right, which was challenging because whenever she looked into it, she saw everything upside down.

The disorientation reminded her of the feelings that had been rolling around in her gut since the meeting with Clairee about the curse. Her experience with the athame seemed like one thing on the surface, but when she threw in the idea of past lives, it turned everything on its head. She wished she'd gotten the chance to bring it up, but Beige had been so concerned about Sam, it didn't seem right to push the conversation. She reached for a smaller pencil to edge in some detail, but was distracted when she noticed Ethan staring in her direction. She smiled. He smiled back. She melted.

He'd been smiling at her like that and looking her in the eye when he saw her ever since their conversation in Katie's driveway the other night. If Marisa didn't know better, she would have thought Grandma Emma had cast a spell on him. But Emma would never do that for the simple fact that Emma didn't believe Marisa needed any love spells. She'd told her often enough that she was beautiful, smart, and worthy of love. When Grandma Emma said it, she almost believed it herself.

The bell rang without warning and Marisa still had supplies to clean up.

"Hey, Marisa. Let me help you with that."

Ethan stood beside her holding her supply box. His arm was centimeters from hers. So close her skin tingled. She started to freeze, but took a deep breath and looked up into puppy dog eyes.

"Thanks, Ethan. You really don't have to help. I don't have to be anywhere after school today."

"Great. I was actually hoping we could head to the coffee house together. Our practice was canceled again and I haven't just chilled for a long time."

"Don't you have someone else to go with?"

He looked at her like she had two heads before she realized she'd insulted him.

"No, I don't mean it like that. I'd love to hang out. What I meant was...well, we don't hang out. I meant you have other friends you hang out with more and..."

He laughed.

"You make me happy, Marisa. Today, I just want to be happy. Can you come?"

"I need to call home first, but yeah, I'd love to."

"Great, meet me at my car in about ten minutes." He finished putting the supplies in her box and snapped it shut. "See you in a few." He looked back over his shoulder as he exited.

Marisa exhaled loudly. She immediately took out her phone and started to text Beige, but midway through her first word she remembered that while Beige had thawed a little in her attitude towards her, their relationship was far from fixed. She knew that in the long run, this was something they'd have to sit and talk about. So, instead she dialed her mother and asked permission to go with Ethan.

"I promise I'll be home by 5:30 for dinner, Mom."

After a few minutes of pleading and several more promises to be on the lookout for perverts, criminals, drunk drivers, and everything else under the sun that her mother could imagine happening to her, she finally hung up and made her way to Ethan's car.

Ethan's family wasn't as wealthy as Sara's but the Martos clan was definitely in the top 2% of Garrison's population when it came to wealth. She slid into the leather seats and breathed in the new car scent.

"How long have you had this car?" she asked.

"My parents got it for me last year when I got my license. Do you like it?"

"Ummm, compared to my station wagon?" she looked at him sideways, "What do you think?"

He laughed again. She wasn't sure when he had decided he was comfortable around her, but something had definitely changed between them since that day in the closet.

"How's your hand?" he asked.

Marisa stomach rolled and she turned in her seat to face him. "What?"

"Your hand? The other day, in the closet. It was hurting, I could feel it."

"You could what?"

He gave her a look of exasperation and shifted the car into first gear. He pulled out of the parking lot and turned on the music before speaking again.

"You were hurt. I thought you were crying from the fight, that's why I followed you into the closet. But when I was holding you I could tell that you were in physical pain. That's why I grabbed your hand. When I did, I felt the burns. How did that happen, by the way?"

"Hold on. Go back to the part where you could tell I was in physical pain. How could you have known that?"

He turned onto the main road and shifted into third.

"I can tell when people are hurting. It's a knack I've always had."

Marisa leaned her head against the soft seat and closed her eyes for a moment. What did she say next? Was she seriously contemplating a discussion of magic and healing with Ethan? Ethan who was Mr. Religion and had dated Sara, the girl who believed Sam was evil. She thought better of it and decided to let it go.

"My hand's fine, thanks. No more burns; all better."

"I'm glad. Sometimes it works and sometimes it doesn't. I'm not sure how to tell when it will or won't yet."

Apparently, he'd gone there for her.

"Ethan, it sounds like you're saying you fixed my hand." She laughed to make it sound like she didn't believe that was possible, just in case she was misinterpreting.

"That is what I'm saying, Marisa. I healed your burns. They're totally gone, right? You should have had a huge scar but there's nothing. I know because I watched you in art class all afternoon."

That was why he'd been looking at her.

"Ummm, Ethan? I don't know what to say here."

"I guess you don't have to say anything." He looked disappointed. "I thought that maybe since you seemed pretty open to weird shit, you of all people might understand what I can do and not think I'm a freak."

Remorse overwhelmed her. He'd been looking for acceptance. This gorgeous boy that every girl considered perfect thought he was defective. Oh, how she knew that feeling.

She gathered all the nerve she had in her body and reached out, putting her hand on his as it covered the gear shift.

"I'm sorry, Ethan. I'm only trying to be careful. After last year with Sara, well, you know how she felt about...weird shit, as you say!"

She giggled. He smiled. She quickly moved her hand away.

"I totally understand what it's like to be able to do things or know things you can't understand," she said. "How long have you been able to heal people?"

"Maybe always? I've only been aware of it since after we took our walk last year. Right after you told me about Sara. You're the first person I've healed other than myself. I started with our dog." He laughed and glanced at her before pulling into a parking space on the street outside the shop. "I can't believe I'm talking to you about this."

"That makes two of us."

He came around and opened the car door for her, offering her his hand to help her out. When she took it, she couldn't believe she was making physical contact with Ethan Martos in a public place. What new world was she living in? Was this another spell gone awry? A dream she'd wake up from? Maybe it was a parallel universe, or she had died and gone to heaven. She followed Ethan to a table where he pulled out her chair.

"What can I get you, Marisa? I'm buying."

"Caramel Frappuccino?" she asked, hoping it wasn't too expensive. Then she remembered the silver SUV. He could probably swing her drink.

"Be right back."

He'd flashed that smile again. She could so get used to that smile.

He returned and sat the highly caloric drink in front of her, before sitting and staring at her like he was waiting for her to start.

"What?" she asked.

"I don't know. I just thought you could help me understand what's happening with me. Why all of a sudden I can heal myself and apparently other people." He reached out and flipped over her hand, looking intently at her palm where the burn marks should have been.

"If you only knew how much help I need in understanding things myself, I'm not sure you'd be asking me."

"There's another reason I wanted it to be you. I mean I obviously could have asked Beige, or gone to Fortunes, but I didn't want to sneak around. No one would think anything of you and I talking in a coffee shop," he said.

"I wouldn't be so sure of that," Marisa replied as she looked over his shoulder and saw the group of cheerleaders enter the premises. "She might not like it."

Ethan looked up and Marisa saw the color drain from his face as he made eye contact with Sara. A confused look passed across hers before it hardened and she thrust her chin in the air and made her way to the counter.

"I don't know why she should care. We haven't really talked since right after she got back from treatment. I thought maybe she'd need a friend. She made it clear that I wasn't one."

"Well, with everything I've been learning lately about your families, I think that may end up being for the best."

The comment slipped out before she realized what she'd said. Ethan gave her a strange look. Anger? Confusion? She wished she was better at reading faces.

"What are you talking about? What have you learned about our families?"

"I shouldn't say."

"Marisa. I brought you here because I need your help. I don't know what's going on with me. I don't know if it's good or bad, even if it's real. I could be going crazy for all I know."

"You're not going crazy."

"Thanks for the vote of confidence," he said.

Marisa noticed Sara kept looking over her shoulder trying to get a glimpse of what was going on with them.

"Maybe this isn't the best place to talk," she said.

"Do you have another suggestion?"

"Are you open to finding out the truth, Ethan? Can you promise that whatever you do, you won't put the people I love in danger?" she asked.

"Marisa, I don't know who you think I am, but I promise, I'm one of the good guys. I don't hurt people."

"Then, come on." She stood and turned towards the door. "There's a whole new world waiting for you and I'm going to take you there."

He followed her to his car and she directed him to Fortunes.

Chapter Thirteen

Sam sat in his room staring at the wall. He'd told Beige he wasn't going to die. His mother had said the future was never set in stone. So why did he have this sinking sensation in his stomach? He had never been a pessimist, but this curse had him reeling. How could his mother have kept such a huge secret all of these years? The curse wasn't some magical idea she hadn't shared. It had been the source of his father's death, directly or not. It could be the cause of his own.

He pictured Beige and how he'd held her as she cried, thinking he could die. She still loved him. There had to be hope for them to get back together. That in itself was reason enough to do everything in his power to figure out how to break the curse. If his father had done it, he could do it, too. And whatever had stopped his father wouldn't be stopping him. His children, Lilah's kids, Ethan's, even that bitch Sara's...they would all be safe from this insane curse if he had anything to say about it.

There was a knock at his door.

"Go away."

The door opened anyway.

"You're not going to die, Sam," Lilah said as she came in and hopped on his bed.

"Of course, I'm not going to die, Lilah. Where would you get an idea like that?" But he already knew. She had to have been eavesdropping on their meeting the night before. He hated that she could have heard something that scared her. "You were hiding and listening at our meeting, weren't you?"

She dropped her eyes to the bed and played with her fingernails.

"It's OK. I would have let you come anyway. It was Mom's choice to protect you. I guess she thought this curse stuff is a little grown up for you."

"But you don't?"

"No, I definitely do think it's too grown up for you, but the way I see it, you're in as much danger as I am, so you should know what's happening. Mom should be able to see that, too."

"But you didn't see it with Beige."

It was like her little eyes saw right into his soul. He looked at her long and hard.

"Are you saying that you think my not telling Beige about Sara was wrong?"

"Momma wanted to protect me. Isn't that the same thing you did to Beige?"

"Are you sure you're only eleven?" He tousled her long dark curls. He couldn't imagine life without her. Thank God he was the intended victim in the curse.

She giggled. "Dad says I'm an old soul."

He smiled, but the smile quickly faded as what she'd said sunk in. Lilah had no memories of their father. "What did you say, Lilah?"

She quickly leapt from the bed and ran for the door. He chased her down the steps calling for his mother along the way. She ran and hid in the parlor.

"Don't be mad, Sam. He said I couldn't tell you," Lilah called from behind the sofa.

Clairee came in from the kitchen, dish towel in hand.

"What? What's happened?" she asked, mildly out of breath.

Sam pointed to behind the couch.

"I don't have time to referee, Sam. Figure this out yourselves." She turned to leave.

"Lilah talked to Dad."

Clairee froze in place before slowly turning and walking into the parlor. She sank to the couch. She looked at Sam with questioning eyes before turning towards the back of the sofa.

"Lilah. Come out here," she commanded, her voice quiet.

Sam watched Lilah crawl out and sit beside Clairee, laying her head on her shoulder.

"I'm so sorry, Momma."

"Sorry?" She tilted Lilah's small face so she could look her in the eyes. "Why are you sorry? You've talked to your father! That's a miracle. What did he say?"

"Mom, you don't understand," Sam said. "She didn't just start speaking to him today. Did you, Lilah? She's been talking to him for who knows how long, and she kept it from us."

Sam felt the pressure in his temples pound. His father contacted Lilah? After all these years of wishing and hoping that he'd connect, he'd chosen her? And she'd kept it a secret? How much could they have learned already if she'd been brave enough to tell them.

"Sam! I don't think either of us is in a position to judge Lilah for keeping secrets." The look she sent him made him feel like a scolded little boy. "In the grand scheme of things her secret was at least motivated by love." She looked back to Lilah, "He asked you not to tell us, didn't he, sweetheart?"

Lilah nodded her head.

"You and I kept our secrets because we didn't trust the people we loved, Sam. Lilah trusted your father even without ever having known him the way we were lucky enough to."

What his mother said hit closer to home than he wanted to admit. Why hadn't he been able to trust Beige? He believed in her and her abilities. It should have been easy. But the feelings that thinking of losing her wrought in his body overwhelmed his reason. This anger he was feeling over being left out of the loop, over not being trusted...this is what Beige had felt. A small seed of doubt cracked open in his chest. He hated being wrong.

"I'm sorry, Lilah." He went and sat next to her and Clairee. "I miss my dad and I want to know everything because I still love him so much. Will you tell us what you know?"

She nodded her head again.

"He showed up last year. It was right after Beige's Aunt Keira left. He said when you channeled her it opened up a way for him to come back. He told me not to tell you. He said you couldn't know anything until it was time."

"Lilah," Clairee took her by the shoulders, "you have to ask him what he found out the morning he was killed. We have to know how to save Sam."

Lilah felt tears filling her eyes. "I did, Momma. He can't remember. He can only guide us."

"It's OK, Lilah," Clairee said, reaching out and taking her into her arms. "Can you call him or does he only appear to you?"

Lilah thought for a moment, "I've never called him, so I don't know. Usually he comes and tells me something weird that doesn't make sense and then later it comes true, or I find out I needed to know what he said. He did the same thing for Sam." She looked at him like he should understand. "The night you fought with Mom about Beige being angry?"

Sam remembered the devastation he'd felt finding out he'd done serious damage to his relationship with Beige. Clairee had been so mad she'd thrown the cards. When he'd picked them up he'd experienced something strange.

"The pain in my arm. He did that? It was a message?" Sam asked.

"He said it was. I was scared. Why would he send you a message that hurt you?"

"Oh baby, you never have to be scared of your father." Clairee turned back to Sam. "What were you doing when you felt the pain?"

"I was picking up the cards you threw. I remember I was holding The Heirophant when I felt the pain because it reminded me of the church services I've had to go to with Beige's family lately. Extremely painful," he said, shooting Lilah a grin.

Sam heard the door open in the outer room, "A customer?" He raised an eyebrow.

"No," Clairee said. "It's Marisa and..." She paused, closed her eyes and then opened them wide. "...Ethan?"

Sam looked up to see the two of them in the doorway.

"Not the best time for a visit, Marisa," Sam said. "Not that there's ever a good time for you to bring him."

"Sam! Don't be rude. We don't know what part Ethan might play in all this," Clairee said.

"Really?" Sam shot back "Weren't we just talking about the message from Dad? A pain that shot through my arm when I held the Heirophant? Who's the most religious guy in school and from a family of any authority in Garrison? If you ask me Ethan fits the card perfectly." He looked Ethan up and down adding, "But then again, he's more a pain in my ass than my arm."

"Maybe this wasn't a good idea, Marisa." Ethan said and turned to leave.

Sam noticed the way she looked after him. He didn't like the guy and her timing in bringing him to the shop was horrible, but he'd already hurt too many of the women in his life lately.

"Stop," he said. There was no way he was saying he was wrong about Ethan, but he could apologize for hurting his friend. "I'm sorry, Marisa. You've come at a really, really bad time. But, you know what? Maybe we could use a distraction." He looked from his mother to Lilah.

"Marisa, Ethan, please come in. Sit down." Clairee stood up and motioned for them to have a seat. "I'll get us something to drink."

Clairee exited to the kitchen and Ethan sat down next to Lilah. Sam snorted. Of course, he'd sit next to the safest person in the room. Marisa sat next to Ethan. They looked pretty funny actually, like little ducks all in a row.

Each of them looked at him with what he interpreted as totally different kinds of fear in their eyes. Marisa was scared he'd go after Ethan. Ethan was plain scared to be in a witch shop, and Lilah was scared he was still upset with her for keeping the secret about their dad. Good, he needed to be feared in the moment. It would be too easy to dwell on how little control and power he had in this whole cursed situation.

"I didn't think you'd be here, Sam. We came to see Clairee," Marisa said. "I had no idea something else had happened since last night."

"It's not a big deal, Marisa." There was no way he was discussing any of this any

"It's not about the curse, Marisa. It's about our dad," Lilah said.

Sam ran his hand through his hair, "Ahhhhhh, Lilah! None of that is Ethan's business."

Ethan finally spoke up. "I think you might be wrong about that. If she's talking about the curse on our three families, I've known about that since I was little."

There was a crash outside the door to the parlor. Sam turned to see Clairee picking up broken glass. "Let me help you, Mom. You could cut yourself."

As if on cue, Clairee cussed, "Damn it!'

"Are you OK, Momma?" Lilah rushed to her side.

"Be careful, sweetie, there's glass all over the floor. I'm fine. It's just a little nick. I was surprised, that's all." She looked at Ethan as she sucked her finger and winced. "You know about the curse?"

"Yes, ma'am," Ethan replied. "My mom told me the story when I was younger. When I started asking questions about my aunt Fran's death."

Sam noticed a strange look pass between Marisa and Ethan before Ethan nodded his head.

"Clairee," Marisa said, "We're not here about the curse. Ethan never told me anything about that. We're here because of what I tried to tell you guys last night...what happened with my spell."

"What?" Ethan looked surprised. "I thought you wanted to tell her I could help her."

"Huh?" Marisa asked.

"Help me with what?" Clairee looked confused now, too.

"For Christ's sake would everyone start saying exactly what they mean and stop trying to hide stuff?" Sam yelled.

Ethan shot Sam a look of disapproval before standing. "Fine. I'll start," he said and walked to Clairee. "Give me your hand, I can fix your finger."

Sam watched as Clairee held out her hand and Ethan covered her finger with his palm. No more than five seconds passed before he was seated beside Marisa once again. Clairee sat cross legged on the floor staring at her finger with a look Sam could only describe as awe.

"You're a healer?" she whispered.

"I guess," he answered and gave her the first genuine smile the parlor had seen in weeks.

"Well, I'll be damned."

"It's not nice to cuss, Momma." Lilah said.

Chapter Fourteen

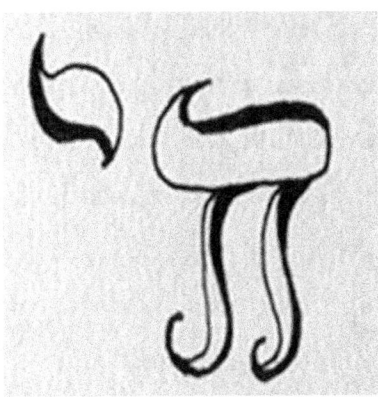

Marisa sobbed uncontrollably into her pillow. Things had not gone how she had planned. Now Ethan knew she was a witch and she had no idea what he thought of her. Why had she brought up the spell in front of him? He hadn't spoken the whole drive home. When he'd dropped her at her door he'd looked her in the eye and said plainly, "I've never believed in curses, Marisa. And to be completely honest I'm a little freaked out at the fact you do spells. I need some time to let all of this sink in."

She hadn't stuck around to ask him what he'd meant. Needing time was no doubt his way of blowing her off. She hadn't even explained the spell in front of him. She still had to go back and talk with Clairee about that. What would he have said if he'd known they'd been together but maybe not really together in another reality or time?

After he'd healed Clairee and she'd questioned him some about his abilities and how and when they'd started, Marisa could tell he'd gotten nervous fast. He began tapping his foot and throwing sideways glances at Sam, whose presence certainly didn't help matters. There were waves of dislike flowing from his aura. Even if Ethan couldn't see them, she was sure he had to have felt them.

Sam, Lilah, and Clairee had been quick to let the subject of the curse drop. Especially after the awkward moment when Ethan had laughed and admitted he'd never believed what his mother had told him. Marisa couldn't understand how a person who could straight up heal someone with his mind could not believe in curses. Still, Sam had managed to get one very important fact out of Ethan before they left the shop. Sara knew about the curse as well.

It seems that the legend of the three families was widely known to all Smiths and Lowells. Sara's family, due to their religious fervor, regarded it as nonsense. Ethan's mother believed wholeheartedly, especially after her sister's death, but his father didn't and his opinion definitely held more sway.

Ethan, who had taken all of his lessons at Garrison Prep very seriously, including the religion and philosophy courses, said he couldn't wrap his mind around how a story like that could be true. And if it was true, he'd asked, where were the Denoncourts? Had they died out? Left town and never returned? It didn't add up. He'd let them all know that to him, the curse was absolute fiction.

Marisa sat up in her bed and reached for more tissues. She would be lucky to avoid looking like a red nosed reindeer the next day. Her breath caught in her throat and she let loose a wail that was so loud her mother knocked on her door.

"Marisa? May I come in?"

"Yes," she sniffed and wiped away the tears that kept reappearing.

Her mother walked over to her bed and sat down.

"I'm not sure what happened, or why you're so upset, but I wanted to help so I called someone," she said.

At first Marisa thought she meant she'd made her an appointment with the family shrink, but before she could ask what she'd done, a familiar figure appeared in the door frame.

"Beige!"

Marisa ran to her friend throwing her arms around her neck. The sweetest feeling in the world was that of Beige hugging her back. Oh how she needed her best friend right now. After what seemed like forever, she let go of Beige and walked back to her mom.

"Thank you," she said through tears as she leaned down to where her mom still sat on the edge of the bed. She wrapped her arms around her neck. "Thank you for knowing just what I needed."

Her mother smiled and left the room, quietly closing the door behind her. Beige walked over to the bed, grabbed a pillow to put in her lap and sat. Marisa joined her.

"So," Beige began. "To be clear, I am still angry with you for working with my boyfriend to try and protect me without my knowledge."

"I'm so sorry," Marisa cried as the tears started flowing again.

"I know you are, Ris. That's why I'm here. We all make mistakes sometime. One of the biggest lessons I learned last year with the whole Keira situation was that there's power in forgiveness. I'm ready to forgive and forget with you. Besides, we have bigger problems these days. We have to be able to work together if we're going to find a way to stop this curse."

"Do you think we can?"

"If we can't, it means Sam dies. There's no way that's happening, Marisa. We have to succeed. So, what in the world has you so upset that your mom would call me?"

Marisa felt the tears welling up again. "Ethan," she managed to eke out.

Beige reached out and put a hand on her shoulder. "Ris, you know what the reading at Fortunes said. You'll be together if that's what you want. You hold the power in that relationship."

"I know," she said, "but that was before we went to Fortunes together."

"You and Ethan went to Fortunes? Why on earth would you take him there?"

"The other day, after our fight, he found me in the janitor's closet."

Marisa had to laugh as Beige wiggled her eyebrows.

"Oh if you only knew, Beige! I thought he was going to kiss me he just hugged me and held my hand."

"That's so sweet," Beige said.

"There's so much more. Part of it I tried to tell you the other night at Fortunes but you were too caught up in the news about Sam."

"Um, I found out my boyfriend might die. Can you blame me?"

"No, but I think what happened to me and this thing with Ethan are somehow connected, I just haven't been able to figure out how."

"OK, well, I have time now. Tell me."

Marisa explained how she had cast the circle with the dagger Clairee had given her and started a protection spell for the people she loved. "And then I opened my eyes and I was by a creek in the middle of the night with a guy who looked exactly like Ethan! But his hair was longer and our clothes were different. He'd been scared for me. He asked if they'd come for me."

"You have no idea who he might have meant?" Beige asked.

"None, and when I started to ask I felt dizzy and ended up back in my room. The circle was still unbroken and my hand where I had been holding the dagger was in severe pain. When I looked down I could see it was burned so I closed the spell as quickly as I could."

"You were physically harmed in a spell? Do you think it had something to do with the athame? You've never been hurt before or had something so crazy happen."

"You know, I hadn't thought of that. I was so hung up on how much the boy I was with looked like Ethan that I barely paid attention to the fact I was hurt. Look, here's the picture I drew of him when I came out of the spell." She pulled her sketchbook from under her pillow.

"Wow," Beige said. "I'm always in awe of your artistic ability, Marisa, but this is a dead-on picture of Ethan...with a few extra inches of hair."

"So you think that Clairee's gift might have been the trigger for taking me to whatever that experience was?" Marisa asked.

"I do. I also think that I might have an idea about what that experience was."

Marisa waited for Beige to continue.

"Remember when Clairee said that she knew the dagger was meant for you? I think she meant more than that she just felt like you should have it. Clairee does psychometry, remember? She can hold objects and know things. I also know, because it's made me really uncomfortable lately, that she believes in past lives and that at the very least she thinks Sam and I have been together before."

"I don't get it." Marisa said.

"What if that dagger did belong to you? What if it took you back to a memory of a past life you shared with Ethan? It's a real possibility, Ris."

"Great," Marisa said. "As if finding out that I did spells and that we all believe in this curse wasn't enough to send Ethan running for the hills, now we're going to bring past life connections into the mix? I know you and Clairee said that the reading meant we'd be together, but I can't see anyway it's gonna happen now."

"Oh, it's going to happen, Marisa. If he's loved you before, he'll love you again, I promise. But you still haven't told me how he ended up with you at Fortunes."

"He asked me to go to the coffee house after school with him."

"Ahhh!" Beige jumped up and down on the bed. "Like a date? He asked you on a date?"

"He asked me for coffee after school." Marisa tried to make Beige see it wasn't that big of a deal. "In the car on the way, he asked me about my hand."

"How did he know about your hand? Is the burn that obvious? Let me see."

"I can't. It's not there anymore, but yes - it was very obvious - a huge Celtic knot in red lines on my palm."

"How can it be gone? Did it disappear?"

"Ethan said he healed me."

Silence encompassed the room as Beige and Marisa contemplated that the boy who Marisa may have shared a past life with, who in this life seemed totally above the realm of anything magic, might have more power than any of them knew.

Chapter Fifteen

Ethan walked off the soccer field drenched in sweat from the after school practice. He didn't know what was the matter with him; the physical exertion and mental release that he gained from time on a soccer field had never failed to boost his spirits, but today he was as low as he'd been since Beige left him on their date at Villa Italiano. Like that night, he felt as if there were things happening around him that were just out of his grasp.

Yesterday with Marisa had been the strangest afternoon of his life. He'd confessed something huge to her. Something he wasn't willing to share with anyone else, not even his mom, and then he'd let her drag him to a psychic's shop where he was touted as a healer in front of the one guy in this world that he really couldn't stand.

It wasn't that Ethan thought Sam was a bad guy; it was just that his pride was still hurt about losing Beige to him. He'd liked her and the betrayal he'd felt when he'd found out what she'd believed him capable of still stung. He'd tried to get over all that by dating Sara. After all, they seemed to have the same values and beliefs.

They'd gone to the same church forever. But something had always felt off with her.

He didn't know what had made him believe Marisa that day she told him what Sara had been doing to Beige, but after that he'd been finished with Sara in a romantic sense. That brought his thoughts full circle to Marisa. At first he'd barely known who she was. He knew she hadn't always lived in Garrison but he couldn't quite place when she'd arrived. But something changed for him on that walk when she told him things he never should have believed but did.

He started noticing her in his classes. He looked for her in the halls. He dreamed about her in ways he hoped she never found out about. He imagined running his fingers through her long red hair and trying to smudge those adorable freckles of hers with his thumbs. He had it bad, in a way he'd never had it for Beige or Sara. But Marisa was shy and she seemed to go out of her way to avoid him after last year. He'd even signed up for art so that he could get closer to her. That had finally paid off last week. Now, he had to add new information to his image of her, and he was having trouble reconciling his attraction to her with what he thought he should be feeling.

Reaching into his gym bag he searched for his keys. He opened the door and threw his bag in the back, almost missing the folded paper under his windshield wiper. Thinking it was probably an advertisement for a band playing that weekend, he started to wad it up, but crisp, neat handwriting caught his eye. On the opposite side, he saw his name. This was a note.

He unfolded the paper and noticed the signature at the bottom. What the hell did Sara have to say to him now? She'd ignored him since returning from treatment; why when he was starting to get somewhere with Marisa would she leave him a note? Did she think they were still in junior high? A memory tugged in the back of his mind. Hadn't Sara been at the coffee house yesterday? As they were leaving, he thought Marisa mentioned seeing her there. If that was the case then the note was the product of jealousy. She didn't want him, but she didn't want him with anyone else either.

He crumpled the note, turned the key and shifted into first. All the note said was for him to meet her at the swings in Grant Park at 5:45pm. He checked his phone. He had 10 minutes to decide if he wanted to hear her out or not. In the end, his curiosity got the better of him. The whole thing could be about Marisa, but what if it wasn't? Sara was someone he really had wanted to make things right with. It had never been his intention to cut her out of his life. That had been her choice.

At 5:43 he pulled into the small lot by the park playground. She sat in a swing on the far side of the mulched area. Still dressed from cheer practice, her blond hair in a high ponytail, she flashed him a smile and seemed genuinely happy he'd shown.

"I didn't know if you'd make it," she said.

"I didn't know if I would either."

"I'm glad you're here. Want to swing?" She motioned for him to sit next to her so he did, though he refrained from actually swinging. "I saw you at the coffee house yesterday with Marisa."

So he was right, she was feeling possessive and didn't like the thought of him liking someone new. Considering the last time that happened she'd drugged her best friend, he should probably warn Marisa.

"So? You haven't talked with me since you came home, Sara. I wanted to be friends. I wanted to give you a second chance but you threw it in my face. Why do you suddenly care who I'm talking to?"

"I don't actually. I still can't believe that you turned me in to my family and helped that witch boy and Beige. But I could care less about Marisa. She's a nobody. I'm not here for myself."

"Who are you here for then?" he asked.

She stopped swinging and stood before speaking. "My father."

"Why would your father have anything to say to me? He wasn't exactly happy last year when I came to him with what I knew about you."

She laughed, "No, he wasn't. He doesn't like you at all now."

"So what could your father possibly have to say to me?"

"He wants me to warn you," she said.

"Careful Sara, you're sounding a little psycho again. Your father may not have believed what I had to say last year, but your mother did. That's why you got help. At least, I'd hoped you gotten help. I'm not so sure now."

"Stop being an asshole, Ethan. The only reason my mother listened to you is because she's friends with your mom. It's hard to ignore the facts from a nurse that can identify the medication used to drug someone."

"Why am I here, Sara? I'm tired, I need to go home. What's this big warning about?"

"My father says to tell you to stay away from Fortunes. That Clairee Reece is a liar and a hoax. He said to tell you the curse is a bunch of bull and she just wants to use you to get back in the good graces of the town."

"So, he only has my interests at heart then," Ethan stated.

"Of course," Sara said and smiled at him. "Nothing good can come from that shop, Ethan. I'm telling you this as a friend. You need to keep your distance."

"After what you did last year, Sara, I have a hard time not hearing that as a threat."

He saw her smile fade. For a moment he felt pity and a small amount of remorse. She seemed genuinely hurt. They had been friends once and he believed in second chances.

"Sara, wait."

She kept walking. It was too late for an apology. He'd had to choose a side and while he wasn't sure about Beige, Sam, and Clairee, he felt in his gut that wherever Marisa stood was right.

Chapter Sixteen

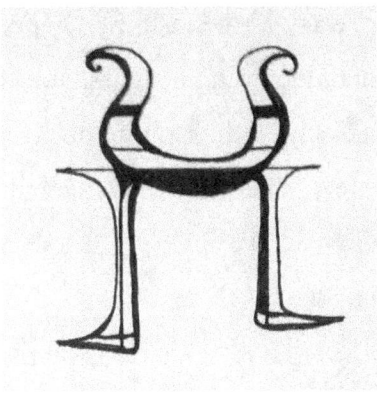

Sam trailed soft kisses down Beige's neck while she ran her hands over his chest to his shoulders, pulling him on top of her. She tried with everything she had to push the thought that they might not have much more time together out of her head. They had spent the last few days talking and talking, and talking some more. She was glad they had moved past talking again but there was too much going on in her brain to focus on Sam's touches.

"What's wrong?" He pulled back and looked into her eyes. "I thought you had finally forgiven me for being overprotective and stupid."

She watched the lazy smile spread across his face and felt heat course throughout her body. Her physical reaction to Sam's presence was the strongest she'd ever experienced. His eyes, such a crazy blend of blues and greens, saw places inside of her heart she'd never thought about sharing with another person.

She loved this man and she knew he loved her. That's why she had been so hurt by his betrayal. But she'd chosen to forgive him. She'd chosen to move past everything and move forward with him, for as long as forward would last. She hoped forever, but with Clairee's announcement regarding the curse the other evening, she realized she didn't know what their future held.

She felt him slip his hand lower to the button on her jeans and slide the zipper down.

"Sam," she exhaled his name.

He went back to kissing her neck as he moved his hand beyond the zipper. Beige felt her body respond. She wanted this. It wasn't like they'd never been here before. In the past year they'd spent hours caught up in each other's bodies. In fact, before their fight, Beige had been ready to make love to him. She'd been sure about her feelings and about his feelings for her and had wanted to him to be her first; her only, really. They'd talked about it, decided the where, how, and the details of responsibility. They'd just been waiting for the right time.

Now that Beige knew she might lose him she was torn. Part of her wanted to make love to him that very moment, to embrace the present and forget about the danger looming ahead. The other part of her was so concerned about the curse and the prediction of his death that she couldn't open herself up to him. She was scared of how much it would hurt if she lost him.

Beige gently pushed Sam away and sat up. "You know I love you, right?"

"As much as I love you," he said. She felt his hands try to bring her back down.

"I'm too freaked out by this curse, Sam. And ...to be honest, still a little hurt from what happened to feel comfortable being with you like this yet."

He looked sad.

"Don't be upset. I still feel everything I used to, maybe even more, but my brain won't turn off."

"Of all the times to have fallen in love with an intelligent woman," he said.

She watched as he rolled over to sit on the side of his bed. He pulled the white t-shirt off the floor. She loved the way the muscles on his back bunched together when he pulled it over his head, the way he tossed his black waves to the side to move them from his face. She felt an intense longing and need in the pit of her stomach. Maybe, when they had figured out how to make sure he lived, when she could know for certain that they'd always be together...

"Beige, you know this is silly. According to my mother we've spent past lives together. This wouldn't even really be the first time we've had sex." He fell backwards on the bed, looking up at her, using the full weight of his charisma.

"You don't fight fair, Sam Reece. Past lives?" She reached down and traced his eyebrows with her finger.

"Don't tell me you doubt my mother," he teased.

"Actually," Beige said, "I don't. I've come to the conclusion that this whole past life scenario makes sense, especially with the readings your mom and I have been doing lately. We're obviously connected on a karmic level."

"Hmmm. I was playing around, but yeah, I believe that, too."
He reached out and took her hand. "So then, the next question, other
than when we're going to sleep together, is how our past lives play a
role in your destiny and saving my life?"

"I have no idea," she said. "Obviously I'm connected
somehow to the cards. I could read them without much help and
your dad mentioned cards to your mom the day of his accident."

"Yeah, but he never said tarot cards." He held up his hands to
fend off her protests before she could get them out. "I agree, tarot
makes the most sense, but we can't assume anything."

Beige stood up and buttoned and zipped her jeans. She let
out a laugh at his expression of defeat.

"Another day, another time, Sam. I promise."

"I know." He reached for her hand and pulled her around to
his side of the bed, setting her on his lap. She sighed as he ran a
hand through her hair, pushing it behind her ears. "I do love you,
Beige Parker. More than my own life."

"That's part of what I'm afraid of, Sam."

"That I would give up my life for you? There's no question,
Beige. Of course I would."

"No, Sam. I couldn't bear that. Living without you, knowing
it was my fault you weren't here...It was bad enough when Keira
died and none of that was even my fault. I couldn't lose you and
there's no way I'd survive knowing it was because of me."

He pushed his thumb against her chin bringing her mouth
down to his level.

"Why, oh why," he said between kisses, "do we waste such precious time talking in circles when we could be making out?"

"We can't make out all afternoon anyway. We have plans tonight. I need to run home and change."

"Plans? What are we doing? Please don't make me go to one of Charlie's soccer games again. I hate watching soccer."

"Don't worry. No games tonight," she said. "Simple, normal double date. Chinese and a movie."

"Double...oh no. No, no, no."

Beige smiled, "Date. Double date. Yes, yes, yes. Marisa and Ethan."

"Not Ethan. I can't be in the same room with him without getting angry about something."

"Well, then we need to see an action movie to release your adrenaline, because you will be in the same room with him, and you'll be nice too. For Marisa."

She buried her hands in his hair and kissed him hard.

"Mmmm...OK," he mumbled. "For Marisa."

Chapter Seventeen

Marisa had never been so nervous in her life. An actual date with Ethan had seemed beyond the realm of possibility before yesterday. She'd thought she'd ruined everything by taking him to Fortunes, but when he came up to her after art class on Monday he'd seemed genuinely upset.

"What's going on, Marisa?" he'd asked. "I only said I needed time to think. You haven't even looked at me all day. I know you've got stranger friends than me, so what gives? Are you just not interested?"

She hadn't known what to say. His interpretation of reality was so far from her own. If his was right, then hers had to be wrong. Was it possible she'd misread Ethan's intentions when he dropped her off after their visit with Clairee? She'd heard what he'd said and was certain that he'd been angry. In her mind he'd been horrified by what he saw and never wanted to see her again.

Beige had said to give him a chance. He might need time to let things sink in. He may have known about the curse on the three families, but he hadn't believed. He'd only just come to believe in his own ability as a healer. Being at Fortunes, hearing things he'd never believed might actually be true, and then learning that she was a witch to top it off? Of course he'd needed time. Marisa had wanted to believe what Beige said, but her head kept telling her it couldn't be true.

Still, there he had stood next to her, waiting for her to reject him. It was crazy. If he only knew how much she didn't deserve someone like him.

"I don't know what you're talking about, Ethan." She kept her eyes on her sketch and tried to play it cool. "I thought you didn't like Fortunes or my friends. I thought I was doing you a favor by leaving you alone."

"Are you for real?" He reached out and pulled her hand from the canvas, holding it for a second before letting it go.

"I'm a pretty honest person, Ethan." As she'd said it, the image of their walk and the spell she'd cast over him came to mind. "Yes," she continued. "I'm for real. I truly thought that finding out about everything, about me especially, would be the end of any friendship between us."

He'd stared at her for a minute before saying, "Apparently a guy has to be pretty blunt with you, Marisa, so here goes. I like you." He'd smiled. "I would like for us to go out. On a date. Like, where I pick you up and buy your dinner? Maybe take you to a movie?"

She'd responded in a whisper. "So, you're ok with... with that fact that I do spells?"

He'd leaned in close, "If you're OK with my healing people."

And that was how it happened. Of course when she'd come home and told her mother the news, she'd freaked. The only way her parents were OK with her dating was in a group, and the only people Marisa knew to group date with were Sam and Beige. Ethan had almost backed out at that.

"You know Sam hates me," he'd told her.

She'd allayed his fears and squared things with Beige, and now here she sat waiting in her living room for the first real date of her life. A real date with Ethan Martos. She could hardly control her excitement and it was making her feel sick to her stomach.

When the doorbell rang and her father went to answer she thought she might get sick, but Ethan handled her father like a pro and they were in his car on the way to the theater before she knew it. She and Beige had decided that going to the movies first might help the evening go smoother. Kind of like when you gave a dog and a cat time to get used to each other's scent before you put them in a room together.

They'd even picked an action movie to give them an outlet for the adrenaline Beige had assured her the guys would both be feeling. Beige was taking psychology and was trying really hard to put her knowledge to good use, but Marisa thought it was pointless. She couldn't see Ethan and Sam being friends no matter what scheme they concocted.

"Marisa! Ethan!" Beige called from across the lobby. "Over here! We went ahead and bought your tickets since it looked like it might sell out."

"Thanks, man. How much do I owe you?" Marisa watched Ethan pull his wallet from his back pocket and settle the debt with Sam. That was about as much as they said to each other at the theater. The next two hours were anything but comfortable. She and Beige sat in the middle with the boys on the outside so they wouldn't have to talk. Sam would talk with Marisa and Ethan tried to make a few comments to Beige before Sam's possessive looks stopped all attempts.

It looked like she and Beige would have to handle this at dinner. The stakes were too high to allow Sam and Ethan to be enemies, even without the curse looming over their heads. Friends mattered to Marisa. These three people had been hard to come by in her life, and she would do whatever it took to make sure that all three stuck around.

"We'll catch you at the restaurant," she said to Beige. "Whoever gets there first should go ahead and get a table."

Once inside the car Ethan looked at Marisa. "I'm sorry," he said. "I tried. I really did. He gives off these vibes that piss me off. He can be such an asshole."

"I can see how you would think that, but I promise he's not. He's protective of me and Beige. Of all of us really...Clairee and Lilah, too."

"Why? What's he so worried about?" he asked.

"I think it might have something to do with losing his dad."

"I remember when that happened. Mom and Mr. Reece grew up together. So you think it's just that he doesn't want to lose anyone else?"

"If I had to bet, I think that's what I'd go with. He feels responsible for Clairee and Lilah, and then last year with Beige...well, you know."

He parked the car in front of Garrison's only Chinese restaurant and turned to look at her. "But he knows I didn't have anything to do with that. It was all Sara. If I had known anything at all, I would have been the one to save Beige," he said.

"I'm kind of happy you weren't, Ethan." She smiled and put her hand over his. She wished she could see inside his head. What was he thinking when his eyes moved from her lips to her eyes and back again? Oh crap, she knew exactly what he was thinking! He was going to kiss her. This was it.

He shifted in his seat and reached to pull her closer. When he was centimeters from her lips he looked into her eyes again. "I'm kind of happy about that, too. Now anyway."

He lowered his lips to hers. They were soft and all of a sudden she couldn't catch her breath. He scooted closer and let his hands move up her arms to hold her face. She was overwhelmed. Anxiety gave way to joy, then desire as she opened to him. That must have been the right thing to do because he kissed her more enthusiastically. When they finally came up for air she noticed the car windows were fogged.

"We better go in before Sam decides to defend your honor or something suicidal like that," Ethan said.

Marisa came back to reality. She let a small laugh escape her at Ethan describing Sam coming after him as suicidal. They'd be pretty evenly matched in a fight. She waited as he walked around to open her car door. Beige and Sam were probably inside and wondering what was keeping them. Then again, knowing Beige, she'd already guessed. Marisa had to admit she couldn't wait for the tell part of kiss and tell.

Beige and Sam were deep into a discussion when she and Ethan entered the restaurant and she hoped it wasn't about her. As they approached the table she heard the words cards, destiny and death, so she figured her make out session with Ethan probably wasn't the topic. They took their seats in uncomfortable silence.

Chapter Eighteen

Beige broke it. "It's time for all of us to get serious, and for the two of you," she looked first at Sam, then at Ethan, "to stop this nonsense and find a way to get along. Ethan, I know you've had a lot to take in and that you didn't believe in the curse on the three families, but I have to ask you. Now that you know about your own power and all of ours, do you admit the curse could be real?"

Ethan noticed Marisa shifting in her seat as Beige spoke.

"We don't have to talk about this right now, Ethan. Let's look at the menu. Beige, what are you going to order?" She was smiling a lot. "I'm thinking about the sweet and sour chicken. That's always good here, don't you think? Have you been here before, Ethan?"

He reached beneath the table and squeezed her knee, thinking he could calm her down. Unfortunately she wasn't expecting it and gave small squeal instead.

"I'm sorry. I'm sorry!" She turned to him. "I'm nervous. I just don't want anyone to feel uncomfortable here," she said.

"Too late," Sam said.

"Agreed," Ethan chimed in.

"Look, Marisa, it's no secret I don't want or need Ethan as a friend, but I am willing to try and call a truce if he is. I think his intentions last year were probably good and I can tell he genuinely cares about you," Sam said.

Marisa blushed. Ethan liked watching her pale freckled skin turn bright pink so easily. "Thank you, Sam," he said. "For a witch boy, which was all I ever heard you called by the way, you seem to be serious about protecting Beige and Marisa. So I guess I can at least respect you."

He saw Marisa smile at Beige who motioned for the waitress.

"OK, then. Let's order," Beige said.

Ethan could tell the girls thought things were good, but he had trouble getting over the fact that he was sitting at the table with a guy who last year thought he was capable of drugging Beige to take advantage of her.

"So Sam," he started, "I'm assuming your efforts at saving your mother last year weren't so successful?"

Sam laid down his menu and glared at him. "About as successful as your efforts to turn Sara towards the light," he said.

The waitress interrupted, "What are y'all having?"

"A pissing contest, apparently," Beige said.

Marisa looked like a lobster.

Ethan had to laugh. He reached over and put his arm around her. "It's fine, Marisa. We're guys. This is how we work out the clash of the alpha males."

The waitress stood there tapping her pen on her pad.

"So, what are y'all having?"

After ordering Ethan decided he wanted to answer Beige's original question.

"I've given what you guys told me the other night a lot of thought. I've also talked it over with my mom." He looked at Marisa. "You know my faith is really important to me."

She nodded.

"It's hard for me to admit that I believe things like curses and magic could be real. The first time I experienced healing something it was Shep, my dog. I thought I was going crazy and I imagined it."

"The first time I read the tarot cards I was sucked into feeling like I was in the cards," Beige told him. "It was seriously freaky, but I had Madame Clairee to help me."

"My grandmother helped me get used to being able to do spells," Marisa added.

Ethan looked at Sam, who responded by shrugging his shoulders.

"Never known life without magic, man. Can't relate."

Beige reached over and hit him on the shoulder. "Sam Reece, you be honest. Last year when you saw Keira for the first time you didn't exactly handle it well."

"Keira? Your aunt? I thought she died," he said as he looked around the table at faces showing obvious concern that they'd said too much. At this point he wasn't sure they could tell him anything that would shock him.

"She did," Beige said. "Keira's spirit was the way we learned about what Sara was doing to me last year."

"I didn't mention that part," Marisa said.

Spirits or ghosts were a lot easier for him to swallow than curses or psychics. He absolutely believed our spirits lived on after death. His faith told him that people went to heaven or hell, but he guessed it didn't have to be a direct flight.

"So as well as being involved in the curse of the three families, everyone at this table also has some extra sensory gift?" he asked.

Marisa started fidgeting again.

"As far as I know, I'm not a part of the curse," she said. "No Goodmans in Garrison back then, and I'm pretty sure I'm not connected to the cards or saving Sam."

Beige put her hand on top of Marisa's and turned towards her. "You are a powerful witch, Marisa. You matter."

He saw Marisa's shoulders relax and she smiled back at Beige.

He added, "A powerful good witch, Marisa."

"Thank you," she said and smiled her beautiful smile at him.

Even with the presence of Sam Reece, Ethan thought he could chalk up their first date as a success.

Chapter Nineteen

Marisa sat in bed turning the athame over and over in her hand. She knew she should get up and get dressed but couldn't stop running her fingers over the Celtic knot and tracing the square, dark green gem stone at its center. She was hesitant to do a spell. What if it hurt again? Or if it took her back to wherever she'd been, and she didn't make it home? She'd been out for two hours last time and lucky that no one found her.

She snuggled back into her pillows, still holding the blade. Had it been hers? When Beige suggested that perhaps what she'd visioned was a past life and that the athame may have belonged to her, she'd felt so excited. It was a much more romantic explanation that astral projection and a stranger that looked like Ethan. If Beige was right then the stranger really was Ethan and they'd been together before. It also meant that her life may have been in danger, because past life Ethan was seriously worried about "Nora", as he called her.

She closed her eyes and thought back to the double date with Beige and Sam. She still couldn't believe Ethan had kissed her! If she tried hard enough she could almost feel his lips on hers, his warm breath and his hands in her hair; it felt so real and so right. She wanted to go on day dreaming like this forever.

She inhaled, and the scent of his freshly washed face and the cool mountain air settled all around her. The sounds of water, like a creek rushing by, filled her ears. She imagined reaching up and grabbing his hand from her hair, to entwine her fingers with his, and a jolt of electricity shot through her arm. The sheer pain forced her back to reality but when came to, she was looking into the deep brown, swoon-worthy eyes she'd been dreaming about.

"I love you, Nora," he said.

It felt like she was two people at once. Marisa's anxiety mounted in her chest, but at the same time, Nora's sweet surrender and acceptance of his love blossomed. She pulled her hands from his soft brown curls and stepped away.

Concern lit his face. "Are you all right?" he asked.

What did she say in response to that? Yes, I'm the best I've ever been, and I never want to leave your arms or wake up from this fantasy, or memory, or whatever it is. Or, No, I'm actually not Nora, I'm from one of your future lives and I'm freaking the hell out because I'm not sure how I got here.

She decided on, "I'm fine."

Of course with this Ethan, as with present life Ethan, that answer would never be enough.

"Nora, I know you're worried about the curse, but now that we know I can heal you, we don't have to worry. I can protect you.

Whatever happens, I'll be here." He pulled her hand to his lips. "I promise."

Her legs turned to jello. All she wanted to do was keep loving and kissing this boy. She leaned back into his arms, then stopped abruptly. Would this be considered cheating on Ethan?

His hands encircled her waist and he put his mouth to her ear. "I promise," he whispered.

She relaxed. Why should she care? If it was a past life they were still the same people and if it was all a dream it didn't matter. She gave into the desire that coursed through her body.

"Come back to the cabin with me," he said as he deepened his kiss.

"What cabin?" she asked before she could stop herself.

He stopped kissing her and gave her an odd look. "Is it happening again? Have you gone somewhere else?"

"Is what happening again? I don't know what you're talking about."

"Are you having an episode?" His voice rose. "Like the other night when we thought your parents had discovered you were gone. You were you, but not you."

So it had been real. He'd known something was off with her.

"Yes," she said. "Definitely having an episode."

He raised an eyebrow. "Well, we need to head back to the cabin for a different purpose. Do you know your name? Are you dizzy?" He put his arm around her to support her in case she fell as they started to walk, but she shrugged him off. He reached for her hand instead.

Here goes nothing, she thought.

"I know you call me Nora," she said, "but I'm sure my name in my time is Marisa."

He stopped in his tracks and dropped the hand he'd been pulling.

"Your time? What year is it in your time?"

"2013," she said.

He sank to a seated position in the grass and pulled her with him. His head in his hands, he sat surrounded by trees colored burnt orange and yellow. She watched him closely for any clue as to what he was thinking and then without warning, he lifted his head and spoke.

"You're serious?"

"You have no idea," Marisa responded. "What year am I in?"

"1911," he answered.

She did the math in her head. "The second cycle of the curse."

"How do you know about the curse if you're from 2013?" His eyes widened.

"I have a better question, Ethan, or whoever you are..."

"Ethan?" He made a face like he'd tasted something disgusting.

"You think I like Nora?" she challenged. "Ethan..."

"Michael," he provided.

"Whatever!" she was starting to feel frustration. She'd been in this experience much too long already. She couldn't help but wonder what was happening to her body in real time. Was she sleeping? Hopefully her mother hadn't come in to get her out of bed. If her mom tried to wake her, would it bring her back? She became lost in the metaphysical possibilities.

"Nora!" He was shaking her shoulders. "Or Marisa, please! Don't leave. How do you know about the curse?"

She shook her head to clear it.

"Because the curse still exists in 2013," she answered, "And it will continue to exist unless we find a way to stop it. I think that's why I'm here." She watched understanding wash over his face. God, he was beautiful.

"What I need to know, Michael," she emphasized his name, "is about what you were just telling me. Why you would need to heal me from the curse. I'm not from the three families."

"Yes, you are. You're Nora Reece. You aren't a Reece in the future?"

She stared at him in shock, "No. I'm friends with the Reeces, but I'm not part of their family. I'm a Goodman. Are there any Goodmans in Garrison in 1911?"

He shook his head.

"Wait," she said. "You believe me? You believe I'm from 2013. Even though I look exactly like your girlfriend and nothing strange happened before I started talking about being from the future. You didn't see anything strange, did you?"

"No," he shook his head. "And you're my fiancée, Nora, not only my sweetheart."

It was her turn to be shocked. "You want to marry me?" The feeling of being the luckiest girl in the world swept through her. She threw her arms around his neck planting a deep and lust filled kiss square on his lips.

"Well, you may have a different name, but you still act like my fiancée," he said and smirked when they came up for air.

"Mmmm," she sighed. She felt warm and safe in his arms. Then she remembered she was anything but safe in this life, in this year. "Why do you think you'll need to protect me from the curse, Ethan? I mean, Michael?"

"Leila Denoncourt's vision."

Marisa's jaw dropped. "The Denoncourts are here? They still live in Garrison?"

"Of course, they do," he answered. "In your time there are no Denoncourts? How is that possible? Without the Denoncourts, there'd be no curse, and you said you were trying to find a way to break it."

"So there must still be a member of the family alive in Garrison," she said.

"There'd have to be," he agreed. "The curse states that as long as a Denoncourt lives, the curse will too."

"But," Marisa started. She suddenly felt weak. "No...I'm not ready." The woods around her began to spin. "I need more time to figure it out!"

Michael's arms went around her to steady her.

"What's the matter?" Fear danced in his eyes.

She opened her mouth to speak but nothing came out. He'd figure it out soon enough, she thought.

Giving into the spinning that blurred her vision, she let go of her connection to the physical body she had occupied. There was no pain this time, though she felt the warm metal of the athame against her palm. She awakened to a pounding in her skull and it took her a few minutes to realize that it was actually a pounding at her door.

"Marisa! Unlock the door. You're scaring me," a voice called from the other side.

She stood, slid the athame under the pillow, and opened the door to allow her mother into the room.

"Finally! You know I hate locked doors, young lady. What..." Her voice trailed off as she raised her hand to Marisa's forehead. "Are you sick? You look like death."

She felt like death. She may have had no burn marks from this trip, but she was suffering from something. Time travel jet lag? How could she explain that to her mother? What the hell had happened to her? She'd cast no spell, only fallen asleep with the athame in her hands. Could it all have been a dream, and if it was did that mean that what Michael had shared with her had been false?

"Get back in bed. I know you have plans with Beige, but she'll have to come here if you want to see her."

She did have plans with Beige. And with Sam. And with Ethan. She doubted her mother would let them have a party in her room, but it was vital that she shared this information with them all as soon as she could. She glanced at the clock, four hours from when she last looked at it. She had definitely been out longer this time. What would happen if she returned? She wondered if returning was even within her control.

Her mother left the room for a thermometer, and she immediately called Beige.

"Hey! I was on my way to the coffee house," Beige said. "Sam can't come though, have you talked to Ethan?"

"He's my next call. I can't come either."

"What? How come?"

"I'm sick. Mom won't let me out of the house," she said.

"OK, well, we really needed to meet with all four of us," Beige sounded disappointed, "but I guess Ethan and I can still try and figure some stuff out."

"No." Marisa didn't even know how to begin to tell Beige what she'd just been through. "I need you to come here, Beige. I'll call and cancel things with Ethan. Mother won't let him in here if I'm sick anyway."

"Why are you being so mysterious, Marisa?"

"Something's happened. I can't talk about it on the phone. Do you think you could sneak your cards in your purse?"

"Your mother would freak if she found us with the cards! What happened? Why do you want to risk that?"

"We need the cards, Beige. Bring them. I've got to go, Ethan's probably there already. See you as soon as possible?"

"On my way," Beige said.

Marisa considered the amount of trust that existed in her relationship with Beige. Even after the betrayal with Sam, Beige didn't hesitate. She asked no questions and had promised to show. Beige had truly learned how to forgive, and Marisa thanked God that she'd found a friend like her. She'd do anything she could to make sure she didn't lose the love of her life. Or lifetimes.

She scrolled through her contacts, found Ethan's picture, and pressed call.

"Hey, where are you guys? I'm at the coffee house waiting," Ethan said as he answered.

"Change of plans." Oh, how she hated disappointing him.

"Are you alright?" There was genuine concern in his voice. How lucky could she be that this boy liked her? And to think they shared so much more than he knew about. He'd wanted to marry her!

"I'm sick and there's no way my mother's letting anyone besides Beige in this house."

"You're sick? Then you need me, Marisa," he said. She could hear the teasing, playful tone in his voice. "I am a healer, right? I think you need a check-up."

She could feel the roses rising in her cheeks. She reminded herself he was flirting with her, but still didn't know how to handle it.

"You there?" he asked.

"Um. Yeah, no exam necessary. I do need to explain what happened, though. You're not going to believe it, but there's no way I can tell you over the phone."

"Something connected to all the curse stuff?"

"Yes," she hesitated, "and to us."

"Really? You and me - us?"

She thought she could hear a smile in his voice and that made her happy beyond belief.

"Uh huh."

"That's intriguing. When can I see you, Marisa? I've missed kissing you."

Her mother had picked that moment to enter the room.

"I have to go. I'll call later," she said.

As soon as she hung up, her mother's hand was back on her forehead and a thermometer dangled from her mouth.

"I swear, Marisa, you're more flushed now than when I left the room!"

Chapter Twenty

Beige sat on Marisa's bed.

"Are you feeling better? You don't look as bad as your mom said on my way up. She made it sound like you were dying."

"She overreacts, but she loves me," Marisa said. "I do have a fever, but it's small."

"So what happened? Why do we need the cards?"

Marisa looked at Beige. She was such a pretty girl. She felt a twinge of jealously before realizing that the thing she for which she most envied Beige, she now had - a boyfriend. If Michael was to be believed...she was loved. Ok, Nora was loved, but if Nora was her and Michael was Ethan, then Ethan loved her, right?

"It happened again." She pulled the dagger from under her pillow and handed it to Beige.

"I thought we decided you wouldn't try another spell on your own, Marisa?" Beige looked pissed. "Now you're sick and you weren't before you did it. How are we supposed to know if you're OK, or if this is connected to the curse?"

"Beige! It's not like I'm gonna die. I'm not even from the three families. At least, not in this life."

The look on Beige's face had been worth throwing the information out without preparation. Confusion followed shock and ended in curiosity.

"What?" Beige asked. "Start at the beginning. Why did you do a spell alone?"

"I didn't. I was holding the athame and thinking about what you'd said about past lives. It made sense that it had been mine before and then I got caught up daydreaming about Ethan and wondering if we really did have past lives together..." She trailed off embarrassed. She'd shared the story of the kiss in the car with Beige, but she had a feeling that what happened between Nora and Michael was on a whole other level. If she'd gone to the cabin with him she may not have come back.

"You're blushing, Marisa," Beige snapped in her face, calling her to the present moment.

"Oh, yeah, sorry. Anyway, this pain ran up my arm and when I opened my eyes I was standing in the woods with Michael in 1911!"

"Who is Michael?" Beige asked.

"Ethan. 1911 Ethan, and I'm 1911 Nora. So, we were making out in the woods and he realized something was different."

"You were what?" Beige shrieked.

"I know, it sounds crazy but he knew that I'd been there before, he remembered the night he woke up. Then I totally freaked him out when I asked about the curse," she said.

"You straight up asked him?"

"He told me that because he could heal people, we didn't have to worry about the curse and my being hurt." She looked at Beige and rolled her eyes. "Which made no sense to me since I'm not a Lowell, Reece, or Smith, and I told him so."

"You're not one of the three families in this life, but you were in 1911?" Beige asked in a hushed voice.

"Yes!" Marisa could barely hold back the excitement. "I was a Reece! And I found out something else really important, even more important than that he loved me and we were engaged."

"Hold up!" Beige raised her hand. "I know this curse stuff has all of us feeling overwhelmed and that Sam's life depends on it, but he loves you? You were engaged! Can we just take a moment. Oh... my... God!"

Beige grabbed her by the shoulders and jumped up and down on the bed. After a moment of celebration, she was back to business.

"What did you learn about the curse?"

"Apparently, the reason we knew I was marked to die was because Leila Denoncourt had a vision. When I acted surprised that the Denoncourts still lived in Garrison, he told me that the curse needs a living Denoncourt to continue."

"Then Sam should be safe!" Beige said.

"I thought that at first too, but why wouldn't Clairee and Mr. Reece have known that? I think it's more likely there's still someone with Denoncourt blood living right here in Garrison."

"We have to find out who it is," Beige said. "Without a living Denoncourt the curse is broken!"

"Beige! What are we going to do if we find someone? Kill them? We can't break the curse that way," Marisa said.

"Can't we?" Beige asked.

"No!"

Beige cracked a smile. "I know, Marisa. Jeez - I'm not a murderer and neither is anyone we know, not even Sara."

Marisa breathed a sigh of relief, but she thought Beige was only half right. She was pretty sure that if it had come out that Sara had been trying to kill Beige the year before, Sam would have taken the matter into his own hands - literally.

"So, funny you should mention Sara because here's what I was thinking..."

She reminded Beige of how last year they had done the spell to try and figure out who the person responsible for drugging her had been. Beige hadn't been physically present but had followed along from her house while Clairee channeled Keira's spirit to help interpret the reading.

"I think you and I can do the same thing here, minus the channeling of course. We don't need your aunt to figure this one out."

"I agree." Beige pulled out her cards and a white candle and lighter. "Your mom's cool with candles, right? The smell won't bring her running?"

"Candles, yes. The smell of burnt herbs from messed up spells? That's why I have air freshener in the drawer over there."

We won't be needing that tonight," Beige said. "So what are we asking? I think we should ask the cards to reveal the remaining Denoncourt in Garrison."

"Sounds good to me. Who shuffles?"

"Since you were the one who found out the truth, I think you should be the one asking," Beige told her.

Marisa held the cards in her hands and separated them into two piles. She shuffled and watched them cascade together. She tried to place herself in the mental space she'd been in when she'd learned the truth, but Ethan...Michael kept taking over her brain. She asked the question out loud again and again trying to distract herself.

"Who is the living Denoncourt in Garrison?" she asked a final time before cutting the cards three times.

Beige fanned the cards face down.

"Draw," she said.

This was new; Beige normally laid the cards out herself. Marisa handed Beige three cards. They had decided on a Past, Present, Future spread, hoping to gain insight into the journey of this last remaining Denoncourt's soul.

Marisa watched Beige flip each card. The tarot was like another language to her, but the card in the past position looked familiar. She'd seen it at the end of her own reading a few weeks before. The High Priestess. It was followed by The Hermit in the present and finally Strength in the future.

"What do you think it means?" Marisa asked.

Beige sat and stared at the cards.

"I don't know." She looked at Marisa, "I'm confused. It's like I'm being blocked. This has only happened one other time...last year and it was with the same card. When I look at this reading the High Priestess is obviously Leila Denoncourt or some other female energy in their family. The High Priestess is connected with intuition, occult power and sometimes secrets."

"But the Hermit," Marisa pointed to the second card, "wasn't that Sam in your readings last year?"

"Yes, but it can also mean a secret coming to light, a need for guidance, someone who acts as a guide...this is where I'm blocked. I have no idea which interpretation is correct."

"What about Strength? I don't know how I feel about the lion next to that woman. She doesn't look very safe to me."

"She's absolutely safe. Strength, or Courage, is one of the best omens in the Major Arcana. That's another thing that doesn't make sense about the reading. If Strength represents who this person is now or in the future, well then they can't be evil. Strength is a card of goodness."

"I think I know what happened, Beige," Marisa said.

"Good! I'm drawing a complete blank."

"I was thinking about Ethan when I shuffled. I didn't mean to be," she held up her hands, "but I couldn't shake him and the kiss, and the engagement. The reading makes much more sense if the High Priestess is me and the secret is the spell from last year that he still doesn't know about. The Hermit would be him finding out and maybe Strength means he'll understand," Marisa said.

"I don't know 'Ris. We should have gotten an answer."

"Maybe we should take it to Clairee? I can go after school tomorrow if my fever's gone. Ethan will have soccer but he could swing by after."

"Sam has class, but he doesn't have to be there," Beige said.

"OK, we should put these away now. I can't imagine my mother will be able to leave us alone much longer. She's a worrier, you know?"

"I know."

Marisa watched Beige gather her things and they said goodnight. As soon as Beige was out the door she grabbed her phone and hit redial. She may not have been able to explain what was going on but that didn't mean she couldn't hear his voice.

Chapter Twenty-One

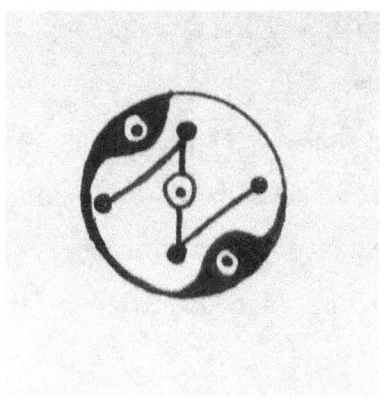

Lilah sat in the parlor waiting for the girls to arrive. Clairee kept moving from room to room picking stuff up and putting it back down again. Ever since Sam had learned of the curse she'd been edgy and short-tempered.

"I know if I send you to your room you'll just sneak down and find a way to listen," her mom told her. "You can stay, but keep your mouth shut. Sam's life may depend on what we find out today."

"I think it does," Lilah answered. "That's why he's here."

"Sam's at work, Lilah!"

"Not him." She raised a hand and pointed at her father sitting in the corner of the room. "Him."

A smile lit his face and calmness sat in the air around him, in direct opposition to Clairee's aura.

"Your father?"

"If you say so," Lilah said.

At that he threw back his head and laughed. She wished Clairee could see him, too. How was she supposed to know if this man was really her dad? He called her Peanut and he knew things about the family, but she knew as well as any clairvoyant that there were evil spirits and tricksters in the world. She glanced back at him and studied his appearance. He was an older version of Sam. He matched all of the pictures in the family album and the few memories she thought she had. Maybe....

"Lilah! If you want to know if he's your father or not just ask him something only your father would know," Clairee said.

"Like what, Momma?"

Lilah watched something pass over Clairee's face. It was a dark expression that she hadn't seen often. Sadness? Anger? She didn't know because when Clairee spoke her voice held no emotion.

"Ask him how old you were when you had your first vision."

She walked to stand next to him. "Well, Daddy? You heard Momma. How old was I when I had my first vision?"

She watched him consider the question and reach out as if to stroke her hair before pulling his hand back.

"You were three, Lilah. It was your vision that started it all."

"What did he tell you?" Clairee asked.

"Three."

"That's right," she said

"He said it was my vision that started it all."

"Oh, oh God." Her hands went to her face and she started shaking her head. "Rafe! Why did you tell her that? It was only a test to prove you were real. Why are you feeding her information she doesn't need to know! She's a little girl."

Lilah watched as her father moved closer to Clairee. When he sat next to her, she suddenly looked up at Lilah.

"You can feel him can't you?" Lilah asked her.

She saw tears in her momma's eyes. She knew Clairee wasn't really mad. She could feel the waves of aching sadness spilling from her body.

"He's there, Momma. He says he loves you."

Her father looked at her wide eyed and smiled. "Thank you," he said. "Tell her it's all going to be OK, Lilah. I have a plan."

Lilah went and sat on Clairee's lap wrapping her arms around her neck. "It'll be OK, Momma. He's got a plan!" She tried to smile hoping it would make her feel better.

"His last plan took him away from me." Clairee wiped tears from her eyes and Lilah looked at her dad, who shrugged his shoulders.

"It was my time, Peanut, but I'm still with her, and you, and Sam. I'll always be with my family."

Lilah took Clairee's face in her small hands. "He's always with us, Momma. It wasn't his fault. He can help us, now, though."

"Why do I always feel like you're the grown up, Lilah?"

"Because I'm special!" she replied.

"Yes, Peanut. More than you know," her father said.

A door opened in the other room and Clairee stood up, smoothed her long skirt and ran a hand through her hair.

"We need help, Clairee!" a voice called out.

"Beige thinks she's blocked again!" Marisa added.

Lilah watched as her mother brought the two girls in and sat everyone around the table. She couldn't actually believe her momma was letting her stay, but she would prove she could handle it. She'd sit very still and watch. She wanted more than anything to be a part of things. Her dad nodded his head and gave her a wink from the sofa. Maybe he was alright after all.

"Lay out the spread for me, Beige, and tell me what you were asking."

"OK," Beige said. "But before we do that, Marisa has a lot that you need to know."

"Marisa?" Clairee gave her a strange look, and Lilah noticed her father leaning forward. This must be important.

"Remember the athame? The gift you gave me?" Marisa asked.

"Of course," said Clairee. "I knew it belonged to you the minute I held it."

"It's taken me to a past life and I found out things out about the curse. Things you'll never believe."

"Oh, I doubt that, Marisa." She shook her head like she did when Lilah spilled her drink. "There's not much about this curse I wouldn't believe. As far as the past lives go, I've been trying to tell Beige about how important they are since we met."

Lilah saw Beige roll her eyes. "OK. OK. You were right. Now can we let Marisa tell her story?"

All eyes shifted to the redhead. Lilah loved Marisa. She loved her gentleness and how she was shy and always nice. She knew that of all the people in her life, Marisa was the one she would trust the most with a secret, just like Sam had after Sara tried to hurt Beige last year. Lilah had been so mad at both of them then, but after thinking about it, she kind of understood why they did it.

"So," Marisa said, "I know Beige told you all about my first experience with the athame..."

Clairee's eyes bugged out of her head. "What? What experience? Beige never said anything!"

"Uh - oh," Beige said as her head turned from Clairee to Marisa and back to Clairee. "I meant to tell you, really. It's just Sam and I got caught up in..."

"Each other," Lilah said.

Beige tried to look mad, but Lilah knew she never stayed that way.

"The first time I used the athame I was transported to another reality," Marisa said. "I was only there for a moment, but in that moment I saw a boy that looked exactly like Ethan and he called me Nora. Beige thinks that the athame belonged to me in a past life and that the Ethan I saw for that brief moment was actually the same Ethan I know now, only in a different time."

"Entirely possible," Lilah heard her mother respond. "I don't think you should use the athame again until we figure out what's happening."

"Too late,' Marisa said as she looked at the floor.

"Marisa, you didn't!" Lilah interrupted. "You could have been hurt."

"Lilah, shhhh." Clairee motioned for Marisa to continue.

"Actually Lilah, I didn't. I was scared, too. I was just holding the athame and I drifted off - at least I think I did. All of a sudden I was back with Ethan, but his name was Michael and it was 1911...the second cycle of the curse."

"How do you know it wasn't a dream, Marisa?" Clairee asked.

"I felt all the physical stuff I did last time. The dizziness and nausea. I wasn't burned this time but I was definitely hurting when I came to. I ran a fever all last night."

"Burned?" Clairee said as she walked towards Marisa. "Where were you hurt? Show me."

"The marks are gone. Ethan healed them," Marisa said.

Lilah looked at her father who was trying to get her attention. He kept saying her name over and over.

"Lilah! Tell them it's all real," he said.

"Daddy says to believe her, Momma."

Beige and Marisa both looked to Lilah. "Mr. Reece is here?" Beige asked.

"Of course he would be," Marisa continued. "Anyway, he's right. It was real. There's no doubt in my mind, plus I got some good info from Michael. When I came to he was telling me that since he could heal me we didn't have to worry about me being hurt form the curse."

146

"Well, when she came to at first they were kissing," Beige said.

Lilah giggled. She loved how Beige could make Marisa turn bright red.

"Go Marisa!" Lilah said.

"Lilah!" Clairee looked shocked but her dad laughed at her.

"You're missing the point...he was trying to save ME from the curse," Marisa said.

"But you're not from the three families," said Clairee.

"Daddy says she is," Lilah broke in. ""Daddy says she used to be a Reece. She was his family."

Lilah watched her mother's face take on a confused look before clarifying, "He said you were a Reece?"

"Yes, and apparently a member of the Denoncourt family, Leila..."

"Did you say Lilah?" Clairee sounded scared.

"No," Marisa continued, "Leila Denoncourt had a vision that I would be the one killed in 1911. Michael, or 1911 Ethan, told me that the curse could only continue if there were living Denoncourts in Garrison!"

"But there aren't any that we know of!" Beige interjected. "So we did a reading to try and reveal the identity of whoever it might be!"

"Hey everybody." A male voice sounded at the door to the parlor. Lilah looked up as Sam entered the room. "You're doing a reading to figure out who the last surviving Denoncourt is?"

"Yes," Beige answered. "The curse can't continue if there are no more Denoncourts. There has to be some way we can use that to our benefit."

"I don't think you want to go that route, Beige," Sam said.

"Why not?" Lilah heard her ask. But Lilah knew the answer before Sam spoke.

"Time to come clean, Mom. You've been keeping all of us in the dark for too long."

Everyone looked at Clairee.

"Lay the cards on the table, Beige. Exactly the way they came up at Marisa's."

Beige placed the High Priestess, the Hermit, and Strength in front of Clairee.

She picked up the High Priestess, "May I introduce Clairee Denoncourt Reece." She held up the Hermit, "Sam Reece." She reached out and touched Strength, "and my little Lilah."

Chapter Twenty-Two

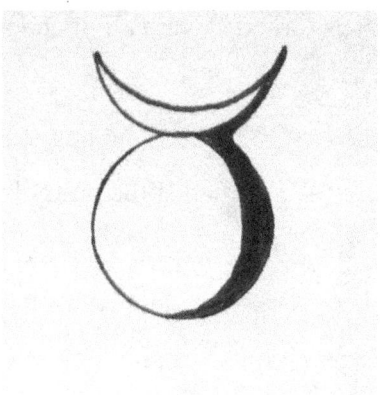

Ethan heard a crowd of people in the parlor as he entered Fortunes. He still felt uncomfortable coming to the shop, but he cared about Marisa, and Beige too, and there was definitely something supernatural happening in his world. He hadn't talked with anyone about it but he'd prayed, and in his prayers he'd asked for a sign. Something to let him know that all of this was OK, and that he and Marisa were supposed to be together. He still wasn't sure about the curse, but knowing that both his mother and Marisa believed made it slightly more credible.

When he walked into the parlor he found Clairee, Lilah, Marisa, Beige, and Sam all trying to talk over one another. They were oblivious to his presence. He watched the way they argued. They weren't really angry with one another, it was like something else he couldn't quite put his finger on, but when Lilah ran to hug Beige, it came to him. They were a family. A family that was opening its arms to him. Because they wanted to or because they felt like they needed to? He wasn't sure, but he was OK with being there.

"What's going on, everybody?"

Five sets of eyes turned towards him and all conversation stopped.

Marisa was the first to move. She hugged him and pulled him down next to her. "We've had some pretty big revelations regarding the curse," she said.

"Great, let's hear 'em." He clapped his hands together.

He noticed Sam roll his eyes and look at Clairee.

"I think Beige and I need some alone time. We're not solving anything here and now, so we're going to head out," Sam said.

"Marisa rode with me, Ethan. Do you think you can get her home?" Beige asked as she grabbed Sam's outstretched hand.

"Sure. No problem." He watched them leave and heard her say to Sam, "You knew!" before whacking him on the shoulder. "Somebody want to tell me what I missed?" he asked.

"Yes, but for now I think I should take Lilah upstairs. She still has homework to finish. Please, Ethan, help yourself to anything you need," Clairee said.

So much for joining the family. It looked like all he did was clear everyone out. Everyone except Marisa, but to be honest, no one else mattered anyway.

"Was it something I said?" He laughed, but got serious when she turned to face him. "What happened to you? You don't look so hot."

"Thanks!" Her tone of voice told him he hadn't phrased it delicately enough.

"I meant I'm worried about you, Marisa. You canceled our plans yesterday because you were sick, and you look pale and really tired."

"I am tired," she said, "but not from any virus."

"OK, bacterial infection, cold, whatever...you don't look well," he said.

She kept cracking her knuckles, "We need to talk about something, but I'm not sure I want to talk about it," she said.

"You were excited to talk about it last night. What happened? I waited all day because you couldn't come to school. How'd you get out of the house, by the way? My parents lock me in if I miss school."

"They had their church group. They won't be home for another hour."

"You snuck out?" He felt a twinge of disappointment. "Did you have to sneak out? Lying never leads to anything good."

"Yes Ethan, I had to sneak out. Beige and I did a reading about some of the information we found out last night and we needed Clairee's help."

He contemplated the situation. Sometimes right and wrong could get so grey. He didn't like lying but since the bigger picture involved Sam's life being in danger, he decided to overlook it. "I've always thought of you as an honest person, Marisa. I hate you having to lie, even if it's for a good cause."

"Sometimes lies are unavoidable, Ethan," she said.

He pushed the uncomfortable feeling that she was referring to something specific from his mind. She looked so worn out. He needed to get her home so she wouldn't get caught.

"How 'bout we get you home and talk there? I don't need you getting grounded before we even get to go out alone."

"Ha," she laughed. "Good luck getting Ozzie and Harriet to agree to that one."

"Who?" he asked.

"Old Fifties television parents...don't worry about it," she said.

He couldn't worry about it. He was too worried about her, and then something clicked. He didn't have to be worried about her. He could heal her.

"Hey!" he said feeling genuinely excited. "I can make you feel better."

"You already do, Ethan. Thank you."

"No, really, Marisa! I can actually make you feel better." He looked at her, willing her to understand without him having to explain. He was still slightly uncomfortable with what he could do.

"Oh!" She looked startled, then smiled. "Right, I forgot. Ok, well, can we go home first? I'm a little worried my parents might come back."

"Definitely. Car's out front. Let's roll."

She didn't say much on the ride. If she hadn't been feeling so rotten, he would have been worried something was wrong. She still hadn't shared what she and Beige had discovered yesterday and the longer she waited to talk, the more concerned he became. She'd said it had something to do with them. He'd liked that she referred to them as "us", but did that mean it was good news? He was into her and had no desire to see things end anytime soon.

He pulled into the drive, got out and ran round to open her door. Seeing her face blanch, he reached down to lift her up. Was it possible she looked worse than she had twenty minutes ago?

"I thought you said you were feeling better," he said.

She leaned against him as they walked towards the door. "I was but it started getting worse this morning. I can barely move," she told him. "My key's in my right back pocket. Can you grab it?"

It was only a small slide from her waist to her pocket, but to get the key he had to put his hand inside. If she felt better he would've made some kind of joke or possibly a move, but it was clear to him she wasn't flirting. He quickly grabbed the key and opened the side door into the kitchen.

"Thank God," she said as she collapsed into a chair.

"Marisa, you need to tell me what happened to you."

"Ok, but Ethan, I'm worried. It has to do with a spell and some other things I know you won't like. I need to know you'll believe me, but more than that, I need to know you won't judge me."

"Believing you has never been hard for me, Marisa. You've told me things I never in a million years would have thought possible - like Sara drugging Beige - and I've never once doubted you. Really," he said when she gave him a funny look. "And as far as judging you is concerned, that's not even an option. 'Judge not lest ye be judged', remember?" He paused and smiled at her. "A favorite bible verse of mine."

She laughed at him, but it was barely audible. "My parents would love you," she said.

He felt the worry inside of him growing stronger. She looked like she could pass out in the chair. He wanted to help her but wasn't sure if he could. He needed to try something soon.

"I want you to tell me all about what you found out about us and I promise to believe every word you say, but maybe we should try and heal you first."

"OK, but why try? Don't you know how?"

"Actually, I'm a little confused about how to start. I held your hands when I healed you before, but you're sick inside - no offense intended. I'm at a loss as to what to hold."

She smiled.

"So, any suggestions where to begin? You're much more into this supernatural stuff than I am."

"I'm a witch," she said.

"A good witch," he said.

"Take me up to my room, Ethan. I think I have something that may help."

He knew it wasn't a good idea to go upstairs with her so close to the time her parents might be home. If they found him in her bedroom his chance of making a good impression and dating her would be over before it started, but she couldn't make it upstairs on her own and if she really had something that could make healing her easier he had to take the chance.

He lifted her from the chair, cradling her in his arms and followed her directions up the stairs. She felt so small and when she laid her head on his shoulder he was overcome with a need to protect her.

"Put me on the bed. It's under the pillow," she said.

"What's under the pillow?"

She reached beside her and pulled out a knife.

Chapter Twenty-Three

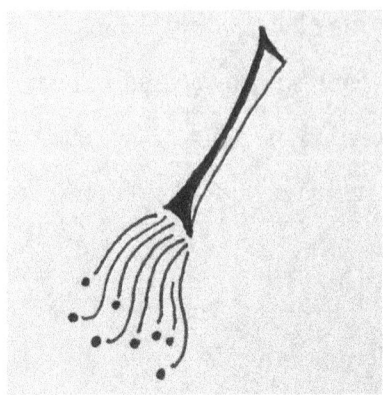

"What the hell, Marisa?" He jumped back, clearly afraid. She noticed his hands were shaking and his breathing got faster.

Despite the sickness she laughed. "No, wait." She put her hand on her stomach and tried to catch her breath. She didn't have the energy for humor. "It's a tool, Ethan! I'm not going to hurt you."

He slowly came towards her and sat on the side of her bed. Taking the athame from her hand he studied it. "I recognize this."

"You healed the marks it left on my hand," she said.

"No." His brows drew together and he ran a finger across the gemstone. "I mean I recognize this. I've held it before."

"You couldn't have. Clairee just gave it to me a few weeks ago."

"How did she get it?" he asked.

"It was in a shipment of new products. She said it reminded her of me." She grabbed his hand and looked him in the eye saying a quick prayer, not a spell, he would believe. "Beige was the one who figured out that it was mine in a past life. It's a gateway object. I've been able to connect with the past twice now."

"What are you talking about?" His eyes crinkled in confusion.

"I've been back in time to our past life. We were together, Ethan. I talked to you, well, not you, but the 'you' you used to be."

He pulled his cell from his back pocket.

"What's your mom's number, Marisa.?"

"What are you doing?" Her chest filled with a tingling sensation; this wasn't going the way she'd hoped.

"You're hallucinating. I don't want to mess around with this. You need a doctor."

His concern sounded real and when he started to dial she used every ounce of what energy she had left to reach out and knock the phone from his hand. She collapsed onto her pillow, tears streaming down her face. Ethan's hand caressed her hair, then her cheek.

"What's wrong with you, Marisa? Tell me what's going on," he pleaded.

"I did."

"Marisa, I recognize this dagger..."

"Athame," she said.

"I recognize this from Sara's father's collection. I held it last year. We were at her house for a dinner party and he took me and some of the other men up to his office to show us his weapons collection. He has stuff from the Revolutionary war and World War II, all kinds of battles. I don't remember when he said this was from, but I know I held it. I can remember him putting it in my hand."

"It came from Clairee. It was a gift. She got it in a shipment." She willed him to believe her. "That's the truth, Ethan."

He was looking at her funny, and for the first time ever she felt like maybe he didn't trust her.

"I held this dagger last year at the Smith house. It couldn't have been in a shipment to Fortunes. It's not that I don't want to believe you, Marisa. I do! It's not even that I don't believe in past lives...enough strange stuff has gone on that I'm willing to stay open to whatever you tell me about, but I know what I know."

The room started to spin. She tried to focus on his eyes to regain her equilibrium but her grip on consciousness slipped slowly away.

"Marisa!" Ethan's voice was the last thing she heard as the soft yellow light of her room faded to black...

...and the first thing she heard when she woke in her new dark prison. Wherever she was, she couldn't open her eyes. Blackness engulfed her and panic flooded her body. Her senses heightened into flight or fight mode though she couldn't fight, or escape. She couldn't move. She willed her mind to quiet itself and tried to assess her situation. She was cold and she smelled wet earth.

"What's wrong with her?"

Ethan's voice.

"I don't know; we found her along the creek bed."

Wet earth on her.

"From the looks of her she hadn't been there long," the stranger's voice continued. "She's lucky Leila happened upon her when she did. Guess her vision of the curse was a true one. I wouldn't hold out too much hope, son."

Leila. The curse. She hadn't heard Ethan, it was Michael. They'd found her on the creek bed. A memory stirred. That's where they'd found Benedicte, but she'd been raped and killed. She was most definitely alive. She tried to inventory the body that shrouded her. She didn't feel any pain, but she had no way of knowing what kind of shape she was in.

"And what if Leila's the reason she's the way she is? What if there is no curse and Leila took advantage of a chance to get Nora out of her way?"

"Watch your tongue, boy. We don't need any more curses on this town."

"All I'm saying is Leila's never liked the fact that I chose Nora over her. You know how women can be. Maybe this was Leila's way to hurt Nora and put the blame on the curse."

It was a good thing Marisa couldn't talk because that crack at women wasn't something she'd let a man in any era get away with. However, this new information she was gleaning proved quite distracting.

"There's no doubting the curse, Michael. Sure as we found young Benedicte's body, her family cursed the three. You're a Lowell. Your Uncle William paid the blood price on this day seventeen All Hallows Eve's ago. You can't question what you know."

"Doc, when the woman you love, the woman you're going to marry, is lying all but lifeless on a table next you, then you can tell me what I can and can't believe. Until then, keep your opinions to yourself."

"You're referring to my medical ones as well? I'd make your peace, young man. That girl's not long for this world. I'll be on my way to let the Reeces know."

Marisa heard a door slam shut and the muffled sound of crying. Something wet and warm slid down her face. Tears but not her own. She felt the weight of a body cover her torso and lips touched hers. The feeling lingered and then disappeared. What was going on? Why hadn't he healed her like he said he would? Then she heard his voice.

"I love you, Nora. I'm sorry, so sorry. If I knew how to save you, I would. I'd give my life for you."

Chapter Twenty-Four

Clairee paced the floor of Fortunes awaiting his arrival. Sometimes she hated knowing what was coming next. To see what would happen and have no control was a horrific experience. Memories of Rafe's death floated in and out of her mind. The phone call, how she had begged him not to leave, his certainty that he'd had it all figured out--each memory like a fresh cut to her heart. The knowledge that he'd never left her and that Lilah could see and hear him, didn't help. If anything, it filled her with a jealousy that shamed her.

Seven years ago, a black hole of loneliness had taken over her life. The only light strong enough to shine in the vacuum had come from Sam and Lilah. They were her beacons of hope, the only way she could still feel Rafe's love. Then last year, Beige had entered their lives. With Beige came Marisa. She didn't understand how much one friendship could transform a soul until she witnessed the love and confidence Beige brought out in the shy girl who'd been coming to Fortunes with her grandmother for years.

Still, underneath all the joy the children brought, she'd struggled to carry the weight of the secret only she and Rafe had shared. Their son, the son they had hoped would break the curse, would be its victim instead.

Clairee walked to the door and peered out. Where was he? He should be here by now. She had hoped her vision had been wrong, but her visions were never wrong. She stared at her wedding ring. She'd visioned her wedding to Rafe before she'd ever met him. She knew Sam's face and personality from the womb. With the good, though, came the bad.

She saw Ethan's car round the corner and park in front of the shop. He crawled from the driver's seat, shoulders slumped, feet dragging. She opened the door and her arms. He fell into her, and she absorbed the wracking sobs that escaped.

"Let it out, just get it all out."

"I couldn't help her."

She stroked his head that leaned down upon her shoulder. "She's not going to die, Ethan. I'd know."

He pulled away, wiping tears from his cheeks and walked into the parlor. He fell full length upon the couch, staring at the ceiling. She wished she could help him understand. She wished she could fully understand herself. What was going on with Marisa was connected to the curse, but she wasn't the victim. She knew in her heart Marisa would recover.

"How?"

"Pardon?" She wasn't sure what he was asking.

"How do you know? Beige called from the hospital. The doctors don't even know what's wrong with her, so how do you? Do you see things or just feel them?"

Clairee paused to give the matter some thought. "Sometimes both. With Marisa, I feel it. I know that she'll be back in this house. I know I'll hold her again in my arms."

"Well, I don't. I know that she blacked out right in front of me. She was burning up with fever and delusional. I know that I couldn't wake her up or heal her. Do you know why I couldn't heal her?"

Clairee noticed his speech getting faster and felt his aura growing dark. She didn't know if he wanted an answer to the last question or not.

"No, Ethan. I don't."

"This is bullshit!" He stood and braced himself in the doorway, before turning quickly to face her. "Tell me."

"I really don't know, Ethan," she said.

"No," he replied. "Tell me everything. About the curse, your husband, why Marisa thought we were together in a past life, and why you had the dagger from Mr. Smith's collection."

A shooting pain ripped across Clairee's chest. When she opened her mouth to speak she felt short of breath. Ethan's arms caught her before she hit the floor. He helped her to the couch and Lilah came running in yelling.

"You're hurting her. Stop it! Stop it now!

"I'm not doing anything, Lilah! I'm helping her sit down," Ethan said.

"Not you! My dad. Stop hurting her now."

The pain left Clairee immediately and she focused her attention on her daughter.

"What happened, Lilah? What's he trying to tell us?"

Lilah rushed into her arms, "Why does he have to hurt you? Sam's arm, now you? Why can't he just tell me what to say?"

"You think my chest pain was a message from your father, sweetie?"

"It was," she said.

"It probably was." She pushed Lilah's hair off her forehead. "Maybe, because we can't see or hear him like you, he's doing the only thing he knows how to do."

Ethan, who had backed away when Lilah came running, stepped forward.

"He interrupted us on purpose. He didn't want you to answer me. Is there some reason I can't know what's going on?"

"No, that wasn't it. Sit. I need to explain." She looked at Lilah and pursed her lips. "You better stay, too, sweet pea. I guess I can't keep you out of things anymore."

"I am eleven, now, Momma," she said.

She looked from Ethan to Lilah and began her story.

"When Rafe and I met and fell in love, we didn't think about the part we each played in the curse. We'd both grown up knowing the story of the three families, but your Aunt Frannie was still alive,

Ethan. No one our age really believed it. Probably because we'd never seen anyone die. It's easy to write history off as a series of coincidences when you feel young and immortal. People die, sure, but not you.

"Rafe and I did talk about the curse before we got married. We still didn't really believe, but he was a Reece and my family cast the spell, so it was bound to come up at some point. We'd hoped that because our children had Denoncourt blood mingled with Reece, they would somehow be protected if it was true."

Ethan still looked anxious.

"Sam was a year old when Frannie died and your mother was ready to give birth to you, Ethan. At first none of us wanted to think about what her death might mean, but my feelings and visions were impossible to ignore. We became believers: your mother, Rafe, me, and Elliot Smith. The four of us held out hope that the mixing of the Denoncourts and Reeces would somehow weaken or even break the curse for the next generation. It wasn't until Lilah's vision when she was three that we knew our plan had failed and Sam was in danger."

Lilah squirmed on her lap and jumped down.

"What did I see, Momma?"

"Lilah, there's no way I'm putting that vision back inside your tiny mind."

She paused as memories of Rafe so handsome and strong, flooded over her. The way he'd held Lilah while she'd dangled her ring on a chain above her head. His soothing voice counting backwards and gently rubbing their baby's temples before chanting the spell to vanquish the memory that kept waking her up in the darkness of night.

She looked to Ethan. "Lilah's vision was what started our search for a way to break the curse. We were desperate. Your mother and Elliot helped for a while, but I think knowing their children were safe took the urgency out of the situation.

"Being one of the only surviving Denoncourts, I thought I would be the one to do it, but the day that Rafe died, he'd said he'd figured out a way to save Sam. The last thing he told me was that it was connected to the cards."

She could still remember his voice. She looked at Lilah and felt a pang of jealousy before she pushed it behind the overwhelming love she held for her daughter.

"After Rafe died, your mother and Elliot stayed away. Without the lead Rafe had been following, everything seemed like a lost cause. Elliot and Marnie turned heavily towards their faith and your mom kept her distance from me. I think that was more out of not knowing how to handle my grief than anything to do with the curse.

"When I met Beige, I knew she was the one we were waiting for. It wasn't a vision exactly but a feeling, like the one I have that says Marisa will live. I could feel her connection to my Sam by something that transcended life and death, and when she read the cards by instinct, I put two and two together. She would be the one to save him. I still don't know how it will all play out, but the tarot and Beige are key to breaking this curse."

When Ethan raised his eyes to hers she couldn't tell what he was thinking or feeling. They looked eerily blank and hopeless.

"I don't care about breaking the curse, Clairee. I know I should since it could be me, or my kids one day, but I don't. I only care about finding a way to make Marisa better and your story, while enlightening, didn't help."

"I'm not finished."

"I don't have time for this," he said. He rose to leave. "What about the knife? How does it fit into what's happening to Marisa? How did you get it away from Mr. Smith and why did you give it to her?"

"Sit down, Ethan."

"No," he said. She could feel his anger rising. "You don't know any more about helping Marisa than I do. I'm going where I should have gone in the first place."

"Ethan, don't. You have no idea what Elliot Smith is capable of. If that athame somehow came from him, you could be in real danger."

"If it came from him? I know what I saw. He put it into my hands last year. He may not like me, Clairee, but he's not as dangerous as you are. There's no magic in the Smith household, nothing crazy if you don't count Sara. If the knife Marisa had is his missing dagger, I want to know how you got it."

"It came in a shipment, Ethan, that's the God's honest truth," she said as she followed him to the door. "Magic isn't the only danger out there and Sara's not the only crazy in that family. It's a bad idea to provoke him. Stay here and wait for Beige and Sam to get back from the hospital."

Even as she begged him she knew it was hopeless; she'd already seen him go. She only hoped she'd armed him with enough information to understand the bigger picture.

He turned to her before he walked out, "You know, Sara said her father wanted her to warn me about you. He said you were a fraud and a liar. Trusting you put Marisa in the hospital. I think it's time to hear the other side of the story."

Chapter Twenty-Five

Beige held Marisa's hand as she sat by her bedside. Sam slept in a chair in the corner. Marisa's parents had gone to get some dinner, but Beige had asked to stay. She needed to be close to her friend. She knew there had to be some way to help her. The doctors attributed her illness to an unknown virus and were giving her anti-viral meds and fluids, but all any of them could do was wait and pray. Her body would fight it off, or it wouldn't. Beige tried to take what Clairee had told her to heart. If Clairee believed Marisa would live, she would live.

Sam stirred from his nap.

"Hey," he said as he stretched his tanned arms and stood to crack his back. "Any change?"

"Since you fell asleep an hour ago?" She smiled and shook her head. "No."

He walked towards her and bent down to encircle her from behind. His nose nudged the space between her jaw and her ear.

"I love you," he said.

She stood and turned into his embrace, resting her cheek against his chest.

"I'm scared."

"I know."

It was amazing how two simple words could make her feel so much better. He knew.   She looked at Marisa lying lifeless while her body fought to survive and imagined Sam in Marisa's place. She quickly pushed the image from her mind.

The curse was still in play. They had no idea how to break it, only that it had to do with the tarot, and in less than two weeks it would be Halloween. In less than two weeks, Sam could be dead. Seventeen years after the death of Ethan's aunt. One hundred thirty-six years after Benedicte Denoncourt was raped and murdered by the side of the creek that still ran through Garrison. The same creek Marisa had sat next to with Ethan in a past life.

What the doctors called a virus may well have been a virus, but Beige believed Marisa's loss of consciousness was more closely connected to what was happening to her when she held the athame. She hadn't done a spell. Ethan had been there the whole time, but she'd held it in her hand and the next thing he knew she was gone. He'd been frantic when Beige arrived.

She had spoken urgently.

"Get out of here now. Go to the shop and wait. I've called her mother and 911. You can't be here when they come, Ethan."

He said he'd been unable to wake her and he didn't want to leave. He wanted to be there in case she woke up, for her to know that he'd tried to help her, but couldn't. He had kept rambling about not knowing how to heal her, that his healing energies either couldn't or wouldn't cooperate. She could see his grief mixed with helplessness and it broke her heart.

"Go to Fortunes, Ethan! Tell Clairee everything. Don't leave anything out. There's something beyond our control happening here. This isn't normal. Go!"

It had finally clicked and he had left just before Marisa's parents and the ambulance arrived. Handling Ethan had been easy compared to Marisa's mother. She'd started screaming and shaking Marisa, trying to wake her. The ambulance workers gave Mrs. Goodman something to calm her down and she rode with them to the hospital. Sam, Beige, and Marisa's dad had followed.

"Do you think she's back there? Do you think she's stuck and can't get home?" Beige asked Sam. "This has to be connected to the past. She learned so much more about the curse the last time."

"In 1911? No. I think she's sick, Beige," he said.

"There's more to it than that. It's not a coincidence that she started feeling bad after going back again yesterday. There has to be a connection."

"I think you want there to be a connection, because it gives you hope. If she's back there then this is magic and we can figure out a way to fight magic, there's even a chance for us to figure out a way to break the curse," he said. "But if it's a virus, if it's an illness, Beige...it's out of our control."

"Yes, but I know that's not true. Your mom told us she'd come back. Arrrghh...this whole thing is so frustrating. I can't lose you both. There has to be a way to discover what your dad knew before his accident."

"Lilah says he doesn't remember. It's like he knows which way to push us, but can't figure out what we actually need to know," he said.

"I'm worried about you," she hugged him again speaking into his neck. She inhaled deeply, his scent calming her.

"I know." He stroked her hair. "I just don't know what our next move is."

His hand stopped stroking and dropped to his side.

"Sam," she turned towards the hospital bed, "What's wrong? Is she OK?" Everything looked the same. There had been no change in Marisa, but when she turned back he was still standing in the same position, almost like he was afraid to move.

"It's my dad."

She looked into the empty space on the other side of Marisa's bed where Sam seemed to be staring. When she looked back, she saw tears in his eyes.

"I can see him, Beige. He's here."

She watched Sam step backwards and sink into the chair. He rubbed his eyes as if they were tired and looked again.

"He's really here."

Beige moved to stand behind Sam, her hand on his shoulder.

"Has he said anything?"

"No, but he's looking at Marisa. It's like he's telling me she knows something. That we have to make contact with her. We have to wake her up."

"That's impossible, Sam. The doctors said..."

"Doctors don't know anything about this, Beige."

It was like he'd done a complete 180. Hadn't he just told her he believed it was a virus? She'd tried to convince him with no luck, and his dad does it without saying a word? Had she been less thrilled about what seeing his dad meant for him, she'd have given him some serious grief. As it was, he was squarely on her side now. Maybe they could devise a plan with Mr. Reece's help.

"Is he still there, Sam?"

"Yes, he's not leaving. Not yet. He wants to tell us something."

"Can he hear me if I talk with him, Sam?"

"He shook his head yes. I don't know why he won't speak!"

"Keira said there were things I needed to find out on my own. Maybe it's the same way with this. Is that what you need us to do, Mr. Reece? We should get Clairee and find a way to make contact with Marisa?" Beige asked.

"He's nodding again. That's good, Beige. We need to call my mom."

Beige saw movement from the corner of her eye. She turned towards the door. "No, Sam. We don't. She's already here."

"And he's gone," Sam said.

Beige felt his shoulders fall and she leaned down to hold him.

Chapter Twenty-Six

Ethan sat in the den of the Smith household waiting for Elliot Smith to grace him with his presence. When he'd knocked at the door, Sara seemed surprised to see him.

"Why are you here, Ethan?" she asked.

"You know what I'm here for."

"Prayers? You want my father to add Marisa to the list for Sunday services?"

He thought he saw her smirk, but if she did, she'd hid it quickly.

"I'll go get Daddy." She turned her back and left him standing in the doorway. "At least I know you can't blame your girlfriend in the hospital on me this time," she said as she walked away.

Sara's mother had come and led him to the den. He walked around the room trying to recall where they had been when Elliot had given him the dagger to hold. There were numerous glass cases hanging from the walls surrounding the large cherry desk. Each case held an assortment of weapons of war. He closed his eyes and tried to recall that evening.

"I see you're a fan of my collection," a deep voice called out from behind him.

When he turned he came face to face with Elliot Smith. Easily more than six feet tall, but with a wiry frame and greying hair, he didn't look that intimidating. When he spoke, however, his voice filled up a room and when he squeezed a hand, his steely grip caused physical pain. Mr. Smith was not someone Ethan relished having a conversation with, but for Marisa's sake he would do anything.

"I was thinking back to last year, sir. After dinner. You brought some of us up to show off your prized pieces," Ethan said.

"Indeed, I did. Funny, when I recall last year, I think of a very different, much more difficult conversation we had in this room."

"I'm sorry to bring back bad memories, sir. Sara seems to be doing well these days."

"She is." He paused, picking up a framed picture from his desk. "Yes, very well. What is it they say? All's well that ends well?"

Ethan noted a gleam of amusement in the man's eye, but couldn't quite figure out the game he seemed to be playing.

"Mr. Smith, I'm here again under very serious circumstances. The things I want to talk with you about are at best, unbelievable," Ethan began.

"So you've fallen under the spell of Clairee Denoncourt and have come to believe in the curse of the three families?"

"I assume you mean Mrs. Reece, and yes, the curse concerns me very much."

Elliot placed a hand on Ethan's shoulder, squeezing hard and guiding him towards the matching chairs opposite the desk.

"Clairee Denoncourt Reece is a charlatan," he said.

"Forgive me, sir?"

"A woman claiming a special power, which of course, she doesn't have. The Clairee I remember from childhood never claimed to be psychic or have unholy powers. I'm concerned about you, Ethan. I still see you at church, but I know from my daughter you've been seen with a young woman who claims to be a witch. And Sara tells me you've been to Fortunes."

"So you've never believed in the curse, sir? Mrs. Reece told me that my mother, yourself and Mr. Reece were all believers after my Aunt Frannie passed."

He pulled at his tie to loosen it, stood and poured himself a drink from a decanter filled with amber liquid.

"Ethan, I was close with all of them growing up, especially your mother and Frannie. I may have been impressionable for a short period due to my grief. Frannie's loss hit me hard, but when we lost Rafe as well, it became clear to me that there was no curse. Only chance and misfortune. People die, Ethan. It's part of life, not a curse."

"I don't want to see Marisa die."

"Ah, Marisa. The young girl's name? Well, I will certainly pray for her and her family, Ethan. Perhaps if she does live, you'll convince her to turn from this evil she's been dabbling in?"

"So you don't believe? In any of it?" Ethan asked.

"No." He set the glass forcefully on the table.

"Then why did you specifically hand me Marisa's athame last year?"

It had been a calculated risk. He needed to see his face when he called the weapon by what Marisa had named it. Mr. Smith rose and walked to the door.

"I'm sure we're finished here, Ethan."

"When we came upstairs after dinner you handed me that knife to hold. Where is it now, Mr. Smith? How did it end up in Clairee's shop?"

"I have no idea what you are talking about," he said and walked over to a drawer in his desk. The dagger you recall holding is right here in my..."

His eyes widened and his bottom lip dropped. He quickly regained his composure.

"I'm sure my wife must have included it in the pieces we sent out for restoration last month. There's no way that it could have ended up in the Denoncourt shop."

"I guarantee you it did, Mr. Smith. and whether you choose to believe in magic or not, that athame is the reason Marisa's in the hospital right this moment," he said. He turned towards the open door.

"Wait!" Mr. Smith called to him.

Ethan stopped and looked over his shoulder. "I have to go see Marisa. You can't help me if you don't believe." He was halfway down the stairs when he heard the bellow from inside the office.

"Sara! Get. In. Here. NOW."

Sara's voice answered from her room on the third floor. Before Ehtan had time to think about what he was doing, he turned back up the stairs and darted into an open hall closet across from the office. From there he could hear their entire conversation, unless Mr. Smith closed the door. in which case he'd just sneak back out. Sara's footsteps passed and a few seconds later, he heard her voice.

"Yes, Daddy?"

"Where is it?" Mr. Smith sounded angry.

"Where is what, Daddy?"

"You know what, Sara. Tell me you didn't put the athame in the hands of our enemies?"

"You mean your dagger? Not our enemies, Daddy," Sara said. "My enemy."

"Sara Elaina Smith! Did you learn nothing from last year?"

"What I learned from last year, Daddy, was to take matters into my own hands instead of doing things your way."

"Going to the Bahamas for a few weeks was a small price to pay for failing to get Beige Parker away from Fortunes."

"But what I wanted was Beige away from Ethan! Your drugging scheme ruined any chance I had with him," she said.

"No, Sara. You did that all on your own with your lack of appropriate remorse. Why would you put my knife in a box at a witch shop? That dagger holds enough power to undo everything I have worked years to put into place. Our very survival is dependent upon keeping the secrets that athame could reveal."

"Please!" Ethan recognized the tone in Sara's voice. It was the one she took on whenever she knew she was right and he was wrong. "It was the best way to get back at them all! I knew Ethan would recognize it and think it was stolen. He can't handle dishonesty."

"Our protection from the curse is dependent upon no one ever knowing our secret and you singlehandedly gave the other families the necessary tool to find that truth."

"What are you talking about?" Ethan thought he heard fear in her voice. "You said there was no curse."

"I lied!"

Things were getting heated and Ethan began to worry about whether or not he would be able to get out of the closet, down the steps and out the door without being noticed. He desperately wanted to wait and hear more, anything that might help him save Marisa, but if Elliot Smith lied about the curse and the athame held the secret to protecting his family, he hated to think what the man would be capable of if he discovered he'd never left the house.

Suddenly the door to the closet flung open.

Standing there, showing no trace of surprise, was Sara's mother. She raised her finger to her lips and pointed towards the stairs. When he was halfway down he saw her walk to the office door before taking a deep breath and entering.

"What is all the shouting about?' he heard her say as she joined the fray.

Ethan didn't stop until he was out the door and in his car as fast as his legs would carry him. He looked back towards the house and saw a tall figure in the den window. His escape hadn't been as clean as he'd hoped, but at least it was an escape.

Chapter Twenty-Seven

It was quiet. Marisa had no idea where she was, but she no longer heard the voices of Michael or the doctor. Icy fingers of fear skated across her skin creating a chill she felt in her bones, Nora's bones. The blackness that hadn't seemed all that scary became frightening in her solitude. She tried to access Nora's mind and memories but she could only see her own. Ethan's face, full of anxiety as she'd drifted away, burned in her mind's eye.

A slow creaking noise sounded, followed by what she thought were footsteps. Who? Had Michael returned to try and heal her? Please, someone help me, she thought. Help me wake up.

A woman's voice broke the stillness.

"So sad."

A hand smoothed her hair away from her face tucking strands behind her ear.

"Michael will be so sad."

The hand brushed over her cheek then traced along her eyebrow before moving to the pulse point behind her ear. The touch was soft but the voice was not.

"Not quite gone yet. Why do you fight, Nora? You can't win. He's mine now. He'll need me to help him through this."

Marisa had no idea who the woman was, but her voice carried a hint of joy.

"A little more to help you along. I'm sure there are angels waiting for a good girl like you."

Something sweet and tangy touched her lips and slid slowly down her throat. It was thick and the taste was familiar. A memory burst forth to light the darkness. Standing by the creek. A dark girl with long hair braided down her back. The girl was smiling as she offered her a drink from her canteen. It wasn't water. Tangy, sugary, thick. She'd tried to spit it out, but the girl had grabbed her hair and pulled her head back, pouring the substance down her throat. She choked and fell to the ground. The girl let go.

"Leila," she heard Nora's voice say.

She remembered her own hands clutching at her throat as she collapsed into the damp mud. She struggled to pull air through the liquid clogging her windpipe while the trees and sky spun above her. Then nothing. Only her own memories as Marisa. Being on the table. Hearing Michael and the doctor.

Fear gripped her heart and squeezed as she realized she no longer felt wet or cold. There was so physical feeling whatsoever. She was air, free of form, spirit. She looked down on the lifeless form. She didn't recognize it. She had thought that maybe, since Ethan looked so much like himself... but no, this girl, Nora, she looked nothing like anyone she had ever known. Her blonde hair weighted down and caked with mud wasn't red and her eyes were closed. She couldn't see a color. She didn't recognize herself.

"Marisa."

She heard her name.

"Marisa!, no..."

She looked down and she was in another place. Hovering above a girl in a hospital bed with red hair pulled back from a pale, freckled face. Chaos reigned below, so different from the peaceful, yet evil scene she'd just left. There were people all around her. They were yelling and a woman rushed in with a cart. Marisa watched with horror as she saw Beige turn into Sam's arms. He pulled her from the room. In a corner quietly standing alone was Clairee. Her eyes never left the body but her hands quickly wove colorful strings into knots.

A wave of recognition washed over Marisa's spirit. She knew what Clairee was doing. She'd been learning how to do it herself last...week? Yesterday? Last year? Marisa realized she had no sense of time. The people were still leaning over her. She looked back to Clairee.

A witch's ladder. Clairee was attempting to save her life. Her energy pulled closer to hear the chant. None of the doctors or nurses noticed the figure standing motionless, but for her fingers, in the corner.

"By knot of one. the spells begun.

By knot of two. strike fast and true.

By knot of three, the child blessed be.

By knot of four, her health restore.

By knot of five, keep this girl alive.

By knot of six, this spell be fixed."

There was more, her fingers kept knotting, but Marisa felt herself being called towards the body of the red haired girl. Clairee's voice grew distant and other voices filled her ears. Sharp pain radiated from her chest to her fingers and she felt her body jolt. Her body. She was back.

"We've got her!" A male voice cried out.

While she still couldn't open her eyes, she felt Nora's fears dissipating and safety seeped into her veins. She let go and fell into a deep sleep, knowing she'd wake up soon enough and the people she loved would surround her.

*****

Marisa jumped as a hand pushed a strand of hair behind her ear.

"Leila!" she cried and opened her eyes.

"Shhh...it's OK, baby. Who's Leila?"

Her mother's light blue eyes looked down on her. Marisa's heart felt like the Grinch's on Christmas morning. She reached up and tried to pull her mother into a hug.

"Careful, careful, baby! You're still hooked up to the IV."

The clanking noise cleared her muddled brain.

"How did I get here? I was at home and Ethan..."

"Yes, you were at home with Beige. Ethan wasn't there but maybe you were on the phone with him? He was so worried about you, too. He's outside with Beige and Sam. They've come every day after school to be with you."

"How long was I gone?" Marisa asked.

"Gone? That's a strange word to choose. A few days." She held up her hand. "I know. I know it feels like a long time, but the doctors have never seen anything like this virus you seem to have contracted. They didn't think you'd recover."

"Don't cry, Mom."

"These are tears of joy, Marisa. God answered our prayers and brought you to us again, like he did when you were a baby."

Something unsettling churned deep in her stomach. The way her mother had phrased that last bit. It wasn't quite right.

"What do you mean, *again*?"

"Marisa!" Beige entered with balloons, followed by Sam with flowers, and Ethan holding her sketchbook from school.

Her ever-present mother, who normally hovered like a mama bird protecting her chick, quickly backed away and left the room. There was something going on with her, but Marisa couldn't go there now. The only thing she wanted was to be with her friends and give them hugs and kisses, especially Ethan.

He walked towards her while Beige and Sam placed the balloons and flowers by the visitor's sofa. His eyes never left hers as he lowered his lips for a kiss. Her body gave a jolt from a different kind of electricity.

"I brought you your sketchbook in case you were bored." He laid it on the table beside the bed and reached for her hand.

"Out of the way, player." Beige pushed him aside and went in for a lengthy hug. "I've missed you so much. Are you OK?"

Marisa shook her head.

"Really?" Sam asked.

"Really. I have so much to tell you guys. Where's Clairee? I have to thank her!"

"What did my mom do?" Sam asked, looking around the room.

"She saved my life."

Ethan moved back to her hand. "Marisa, I know this might be scary for you to hear, but you flatlined. The doctors and nurses - they saved you. It was touch and go for almost the whole night."

"I saw them. I remember that, but Clairee was the one who saved me. I watched her stand in that corner right there and weave a witch's ladder. I heard her chant the spell."

Ethan looked frustrated.

"Can't you for once believe anything happens the normal way? We were all out in the lobby when it happened, Marisa. I've come to believe in a lot since we met, but it was science and medicine that saved your life," he said.

"I thought it was God, church boy," Sam said. He leaned against the wall on the opposite side of the bed. "He's right though, Risa. Mom was at home with Lilah when it happened."

"But it was so real. It was all so real...Leila, the poison, you not being able to heal me." She looked at Ethan.

"When you're feeling better we'll sit down and work through what happened, Marisa. Some of it may have been connected to the athame," Beige said. "And if it was, we have to start putting the pieces together before next weekend." She reached for Sam's hand.

"What's next weekend?" she asked.

"Samhain," Ethan answered. "Or, as the locals call it - Halloween."

Marisa's eyes widened, "E! Where'd you learn to talk witch?"

Sam started to laugh. "Lilah's been teaching him," he said.

"I've got some stuff to tell you about the knife, too," Ethan added. "You'll never guess how it got to Fortunes."

"How?" Marisa asked.

"Our old friend, Sara," he said. "She was setting you up, Marisa. She knew I'd seen the dagger at her house and thought that I would think you or Clairee stole it."

"Didn't you? For a second?" she asked.

"No! Why would you think that?"

She lowered her eyes to the floor, but he reached out and turned her face to his.

"I know you would never lie to me, Marisa."

The churning in her stomach intensified and a heavy cloud of guilt settled on her shoulders.

"We'll leave you guys to talk," Beige said. She grabbed Sam's hand.

"Ethan, there's something I should have told you a while ago," she said.

Chapter Twenty-Eight

Beige dropped onto the bean bag on the floor of Sam's room. He followed her lead, squeezing in next to her.

"Hey, you're squishing me."

"Good," he said and leaned closer. The bean bag molded to their forms as they sank and his body covered hers.

"I'm glad I'm not a part of that conversation we just left," he said. He ran a hand through her dark brown hair. He loved it when she wore it long and loose. He leaned forward and kissed her. Knowing that his time with her could be limited, he didn't want to waste a moment. "I love you, Beige. You're my best friend and the best thing that's ever happened to me."

"I love you, too."

He felt her hand caress his cheek. He loved the way she looked at him. There was total trust and surrender in her gaze. He couldn't believe he'd almost ruined it all because of Sara Smith.

"Can you believe a year later we're still dealing with her?" Beige asked.

He moved in to kiss her neck, placing his hand on her hip. "Don't kill the moment for me, Beige." He moved back to her lips and kissed her more deeply.

"But there's got to be more going on here than her obsession with Ethan." She pushed him back and drew her brows together, "I feel like it's all got to be connected somehow. The families are all connected...well, not mine but all of yours."

He laid his head against her chest. He could feel her heartbeat increasing.

"I kinda wish we hadn't rushed out of there," she said. "The two of them probably have all the information we need to save you. Marisa has to know more since she was gone so long and if we add that to the stuff Ethan discovered, it has to be enough. I can't believe he got Sara to confess to setting us all up."

He shifted his head and looked up at her. "No, he didn't say she confessed. I can't imagine that girl telling the truth to anyone."

"Well, how he found out doesn't matter. Do you think she had any idea what she was doing when she gave Marisa the athame, or was she setting us all up to look like thieves?"

Sam sat up and scooted off the bean bag onto the floor. "We're not making out, are we?"

Beige shook her head. "I can't think of anything else."

He pushed his disappointment to the back of his mind. Maybe it was better that they didn't go any further in their physical relationship. It would be selfish of him to be with her when he might be dead soon. Add to that the fact that no matter how careful they were, he couldn't risk bringing any kids into the world while the curse hung over their heads. They really did need to start trying to put the pieces together.

At the thought of kids and Beige, Sam felt a sharp twinge in his heart. He'd always assumed they'd have a family. He could see their future as clearly as their present, but this curse threatened everything he was trying to build. Would he become a police officer? Would they ever have a wedding? He felt his heartbeat quicken at the thought of all the possible losses.

He took a deep breath and focused in on Beige's eyes. The love and concern that looked back at him anchored his soul. He resolved to do whatever it took to stay alive. He would survive and they'd have their family.

"OK, well, if we're not making out, then in my opinion, yes, I think she was just setting us up. If there's one thing I've learned from observing Sara this past year, it's that she truly believes magic is evil. If she knew that dagger held any mystical properties she would never have touched it," he said.

"I agree," Beige said. "So, it was a coincidence that the athame triggered Marisa's past life experiences. No one could have guessed they would physically affect her that way."

"But, Mr. Smith still could have known what the athame did," he said. "I don't believe he's the paragon of religion he seems to be. Especially after knowing he believed in the curse when Ethan's aunt died."

"I guess he could have known, but I spent my whole life up until last year at their house, Sam. There's nothing to give anyone supernatural ideas anywhere in that house. Where do you think Sara learned to be so freaked out by all this stuff? Her parents taught her!"

"What about this collection the athame came from? Did you ever see it?"

"Sure, he's got cases of weapons in the den. Some of them are ancient, but I never got any kind of vibes from them," she said. "Not that I'd have been tuned into what vibes felt like back then."

He ran his hand through his curls.

"I need a haircut," he said.

Beige laughed at him. "There's that Sam Reece laser sharp focus I love so much."

"I was laser focused earlier. But you derailed my efforts at seduction."

He watched her stiffen. "I'm sorry for wanting you to live more than wanting you in this moment," she said.

He'd pissed her off, but maybe that was for the better. If she was a little pissed things couldn't get too serious. He could control his desire for her better that way.

"My mom wants to meet with you, me, and Ethan on Wednesday after school. I think you should be the one to call and tell him." He changed the subject.

"What? One double date's not enough make you best buds?"

She was teasing him. That was a good sign.

"OK," she said. "I'll make sure I get him here. Why doesn't she want to include Marisa?"

"She doesn't want to stress her out any more than she has too. She says when she did the healing spell in her room that night she connected with Marisa when she slept. She was able to extract the information she needed about what had happened."

"I think I'm going back tonight anyway. I need to hear it in her own words and I'm sure she needs to tell someone. Not to mention that I can't imagine it was easy when she fessed up to Ethan about last year," she said.

He watched her stand and stretch. He couldn't imagine life without her. Would he follow her around for the rest of her life if the curse killed him? He wondered. That's what his dad had done. All those times Sam had felt like that his dad had never left had been spot on. Rafe Reece never had.

"What are you thinking?" she asked.

He smiled. "How much my dad would've liked you."

"What do you mean would have? I'm sure he does!"

He let that thought settle over him before he stood and gave her one last kiss for the road. It was nice to know for sure that his dad was with him. That he might actually get the chance to talk with him at some point. Rafe had died trying to save him from this curse, and he was going to do everything he could to live, so that death wouldn't be in vain.

"I love the fact that he's still with you, Sam. Really, I do, but next time you see him can you make sure he's not always around? I mean, we don't see him or anything, but how can we know he's not in the room?"

"I'm pretty sure I'll be able to see him from now on, but I'll be sure to let him know you'd like some private time to take advantage of me," he said.

"That's not what I said! Don't you dare tell him that, Sam."

"How are you gonna stop me?" He lifted a strand of her hair from her shoulder and began to twirl it round his finger, pulling her closer.

"I'll ask Ethan over as often as possible," she whispered.

"I'll have think it over. I've started to like Ethan, you know."

Her eyes widened and she asked, "Really?"

"No," he said and kissed her again before pushing her out the door.

Chapter Twenty-Nine

Why did he have to be so good looking? Marisa's eyes roamed his coffee colored curls that hung just below his square jaw. His hand held hers and for one moment in time, everything seemed right. She knew as soon as Beige and Sam left the room, though, that her dreams of a real romance with Ethan Martos would be as dead as Nora Reece in 1911. If there was one thing a relationship with him wouldn't survive, it was deceit, and now she had to tell him their friendship had been built on it.

"What is it, Marisa? I can tell you're scared to tell me something."

She nodded her head. Why? Why when she finally had everything she'd hoped for - a best friend, a family, a purpose, and a love life - did she have to go and destroy it with this truth? She contemplated keeping the secret a while longer, but knew that after everything they'd been through together as Michael and Nora, and now as Marisa and Ethan, he deserved the truth.

"Come on, Marisa, how horrible can it be? Were you a man in your past life? Am I in love with a dude?"

An uncomfortable quiet filled the room. Did he realize what he'd said? Had it been a slip of the tongue? Surely he couldn't be in love with her? In a past life, maybe. When she was the brave and beautiful Nora, but how could he love her like this? It must have been a mistake. She looked away, his intense gaze burning her skin like the summer sun. She couldn't look him in the eye.

"I'm sorry," he said and let go of her hand.

"It's fine, don't worry about it. We all say things by accident sometimes. I didn't believe you. We're OK...and even if I did believe you and even if you had meant it..."

"Marisa, you're rambling."

"...even if you did mean it, the thing I have to tell you next would probably make you change your mind and leave me anyway. I'm the one who's sorry, Ethan. So, so, seriously sorry."

Surprise and curiosity coursed through her when she felt him take her hand again.

"You think I said I love you by accident?" She heard laughter in his voice. Was he making fun of her? She didn't think she could handle that.

"I always say what I mean, Marisa. I thought you were going to die. That puts a lot of things into perspective," he said.

"You love me?"

He nodded.

She pinched herself under the hospital blanket to make sure she was awake. Ethan Martos just declared his love for her. And now she had to choose to do the right thing because she loved him. With all her heart, she loved him. She had to tell him the truth and set him free from this relationship built on her lie. It was the hardest thing she'd ever had to do.

"I love you, too."

He started to move towards her. He was going to kiss her, but she threw out her hand and pushed him back.

"What? What is this thing we have to talk about that has you so freaked out?" he asked.

"Do you remember our walk when I told you about Sara? The one where you've said you believed me even though you didn't know why?"

She watched his eyes narrow. He was too smart not to figure this out. He had to know where she was going.

"Well," she continued, "you didn't believe me at first and I knew it was so important for Beige's safety that you did believe. I kind of, well, sort of..."

"You put a spell on me," he said.

His face was void of any emotion. She couldn't tell if he was angry or sad, but knowing Ethan the way she did, she thought disappointment would be the first thing he expressed.

"You put a spell on me!"

This time he sounded incredulous. He stood and turned to face the window for a good minute or two. The anticipation of the breakup ate away at her insides.

"I'm so sorry, Ethan. I know this changes everything."

He turned to her.

"You know it was wrong, right?"

"I do," she confessed.

"Would you do it again? Should I be worried that my feelings for you aren't really my own?"

"No!" she said. "I didn't want to do it to you then. I was so worried about saving Beige! I would never play with your feelings. I couldn't make you love me if I tried and I would never, never try!"

He walked towards the bed and reached down to gently touch her cheek. He leaned over and lightly put his lips to hers. What in the world was happening? He should have been stomping out of the room and slamming the door. He should be telling her he never wanted to talk with her again.

"That's the Marisa I love. The girl who does no harm. I know that's part of your witch's code, too. Kind of like a doctor's. Maybe since I'm a healer we have that in common."

He held her hand and brushed his thumb back and forth across her knuckles.

"I don't understand," she said.

"Well, let's see if we can clear things up for you."

She couldn't believe this was happening. Was he forgiving her? Was there a chance they would actually make it through this?

"Am I upset that you put a spell on me without my knowledge? Absolutely," he said. "Do I understand why you did it? A hundred percent...I was so pissed at Beige and Sam that I never would have seen reason about Sara."

"But I still shouldn't have..."

"Shhh..." He put his finger to her lips. "You're sorry. You know you were wrong and it won't happen again. I almost lost you. That makes this spell that happened last year seem pretty insignificant, ya know?"

"I know," she said.

"Then there's the fact that I love you. And, I love that you're blushing right now," he laughed as he said it. "I love you, Marisa. Do I need to remind you what love is besides patient and kind?"

"Maybe," she said, wanting to hear him tell her more of his feelings.

"It keeps no record of being wronged. It does not rejoice about injustice but rejoices whenever the truth wins out."

"Corinthians," she said.

"Love never gives up, never loses faith, is always hopeful, and endures through every circumstance." He leaned down to kiss her again. "What kind of love would ours be if I gave up on us because of something you've already punished yourself for?"

She kissed him back and raised her arms to pull him closer. "Oh!"

A high pitched voice sounded at the door.

"Um, excuse me. I'm sorry. I guess I should have...Marisa, how are you feeling?" her mother asked.

"Hello, Mrs. Goodman. Marisa and I were just - we uh...well, did I tell you I'm really happy Marisa's OK?"

Marisa looked at her mother who couldn't seem to figure out what to do with her hands.

"It's OK, Mom. Ethan's my boyfriend."

She couldn't tell if the shock on her mother's face was a continuation from the kiss or an entirely new emotion, but she cared enough about her to know that she should probably get Ethan to go.

"Ethan was leaving, that was a kiss goodbye," she said.

"Oh, well, Ethan. Thank you for being here. I'm very thankful for all the care you've shown Marisa."

"It's no problem, Mrs. Goodman. Like Marisa said," he turned and winked at her, "I'm her boyfriend."

"Yes, but Ethan," her mother stopped him on the way out by grabbing his shoulder, "I wouldn't tell Mr. Goodman about that quite yet. Understood?"

"Absolutely," he agreed.

Chapter Thirty

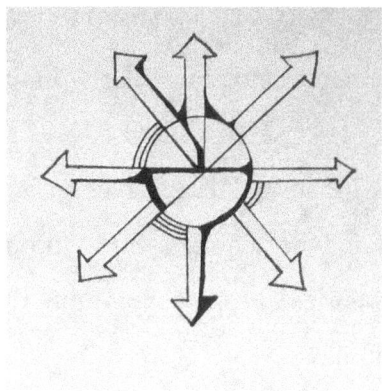

Lilah brought the tea in from the kitchen and placed it in the center of the table before going back for the cups. Today was the big meeting. There were only five days left until Halloween and they had to figure out what they needed to do to save Sam. They had to! Everyone was already seated in the parlor and listening to Clairee's story that she'd told Ethan the night Marisa went to the hospital. When she finished, Lilah sat next to her. She noticed her father in the corner of the room. She liked that he was there. Somehow over the course of the past few weeks she'd come to believe in him and love him.

"I'm not sure what we can do without Marisa," Beige said.

"We don't need Marisa," Clairee said. "I already know her story."

"When did you get to talk with her?" Ethan asked. "One of us was always there after she woke up, and her parents never would have let you in the room."

Clairee's head turned sharply towards Ethan.

"No offense." He raised his hands. "I'm sorry for the way I behaved that night. I was scared and needed someone to blame. Marisa means everything to me now. She's changed my whole view of the world."

"None taken, Ethan." Clairee's eyes softened. "I was in the room when she died and the healing spell I worked allowed me to connect with her memories. I know everything that happened to her on her trip back in time."

"So you were there? She said you were but I didn't believe it was possible," Ethan said.

"I would think you've learned by now that impossible is a word to remove from your vocabulary," Sam said to Ethan. Turning to his mom, he continued, "Marisa said you saved her, but we didn't see you."

Lilah watched Clairee. Sometimes she was amazed at what her mother could do. She'd saved Marisa. How had she done it without anyone knowing she was there? Did her dad help her? She looked to the corner where Rafe sat smiling and nodding.

"Dad helped her!" Lilah said, interrupting the questions coming from Beige and Sam.

"Lilah! No, he just put the idea in my head, honey. He didn't help me do the spell. I've still not been able to see or feel your father."

"Hold on," Ethan said. "You're telling us that you saved Marisa's life with the help of your dead husband? It had nothing to do with the medical team that we all actually saw in the room?"

Lilah could tell Ethan was still having trouble believing.

"It's OK, Ethan," she said. "You're going to believe everything before you leave here tonight!"

Clairee gave her a funny look.

"Lilah, what do you know?" she asked.

"I saw it in my vision. You're gonna hypnotize Ethan!"

Clairee covered her eyes with her hand. Lilah didn't understand why everyone was looking at her like they were. It looked like Ethan was starting to sweat. Maybe she'd made him nervous.

"You kind of need to prep someone like Ethan for this kind of thing, Peanut," her dad said. "Ethan's not so sure about any of this yet."

Lila walked over to Ethan and put both hands on his cheeks. She looked him square in the eye before speaking.

"Ethan! You've got to do this. I know you don't believe everything yet, but my dad says you will! I promise. You have to trust my momma. This is the only way to save my brother! Please help us."

Ethan reached up and removed her hands from his cheeks.

"Little Lilah, did you just put a spell on me?" he said.

She looked at him confused, "No. I don't do spells. That's Marisa."

"It's a figure of speech, kiddo." He looked around the room, his eyes finally resting on Clairee. "What do we have to do? I've never been hypnotized before. I'm not sure I can be."

"Are you sure you want to be, Ethan? I'll be trying to take you back to 1911. We know that Marisa was Nora back then and we're assuming that you're Michael."

"I'm good with that," he said. "As good as I can be, I guess."

"You need to be certain, Ethan. It's not without some risk," Clairee said.

"You're only taking him back to his own memories though, right, Clairee?" Beige asked. "With Marisa and the athame there was magic involved...this is straight up psychology."

"Well, no." Clairee said. "I can't say this doesn't involve anything supernatural. This ring's been in my family for over a hundred years. It's a talisman so there's some magic involved."

Lilah looked at the ring. She remembered it dangling above her face when she was little.

"You couldn't remember that, Peanut," her dad read her thoughts.

"Yes, I do," she told him in her mind.

"It'll work," Lilah told everyone. "Like when they hypnotized me and took away my memory of how Sam is going to die."

She heard Beige gasp and saw Sam take her hand. Her momma shook her head.

"Lilah, after we save your brother's life you and I are going to have a long talk about when and how to tell people things," Clairee said.

"What? I'm just telling it like it is."

Beige and Sam laughed. Ethan joined in. Only her momma kept a straight face, but she thought she noticed the corner of her mouth twitching.

"OK, Clairee," Ethan said, "but you're not taking any memories away, right? Only helping me access new ones?"

"Exactly. The life you shared with Marisa is somewhere in your soul memory. We should be able to regress you to your former self and learn what happened after Nora's death. I want to know if Michael ever figured out what happened." She paused and thought about something before she continued, "I have one more thing that bothers me about Marisa's story that I need you to try and clarify."

Clairee removed the opal ring from her left hand and placed it on the chain she took from her neck.

"What?" Ethan asked.

"Nora was murdered. We know Leila poisoned her, but history suggests that the curse brings about tragic accidental death. We need to know if Nora was the actual victim of the curse in 1911 or if it was all just some terrible coincidence of timing," Clairee explained.

"Oh my God," Beige said. "You don't think Marisa's death was part of the curse?"

"I don't," she confirmed. "Now, is everyone comfortable? Once we start we can't be interrupted."

Lilah watched everyone nod their heads.

"Ethan, I need you to begin by focusing on your breathing. Breathe in deeply for a count of three and then out for a count of three."

While Clairee continued to instruct Ethan, Lilah moved to where her dad was sitting and slid down the wall next to him.

"So, if you had a vision, Peanut, then you know we're about to be interrupted," he said.

She nodded her head and spoke back to him in her mind. "Yep, she can't do it without you, even if she thinks she can. Do you think Sam will be able to handle it?"

"I hope so," her dad said. "I think this is key to saving Sam. It's the only way I can think of to get the necessary information out there."

"I don't understand why you can't just tell us," Lilah thought.

"Me either, baby. It's like when I go to find the words to tell you what I know, they're not there. I don't know why."

"I guess it's OK," she thought, "this way will work well enough."

"And here we go," he said as the front door slammed and loud footsteps stomped through the shop.

Chapter Thirty-One

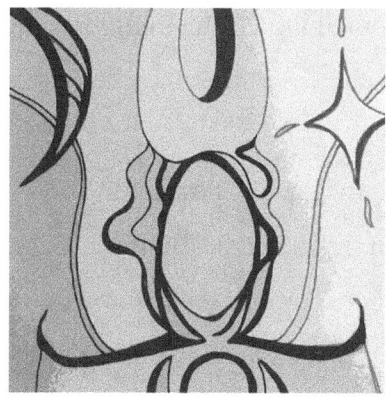

"You were really going to do this without me!" Marisa growled in her meanest voice, at least she tried to make it her meanest voice. She wasn't very comfortable expressing anger.

They all stared up at her in shock. All except Lilah, who seemed to be involved in a mental game of tennis with the wall.

"Honey! You shouldn't be out of bed!" Clairee rose to her feet and rushed to bring Marisa to the couch. Ethan scooted over to make room and immediately put his arm around her. She shrugged him off and continued her rant.

"I asked you a question. Were you really," she looked at each one of them as she spoke, "after everything I've been through, going to leave me out of something I've already risked my life for?"

"How did you know we were here?" Beige asked.

She looked to Ethan who ran his hands through his hair and fell back against the couch. He sighed and crossed his arms.

"I am lucky enough to have a boyfriend who doesn't believe in lying," she said. "You were going to leave me out?"

The hurt under the anger came to the surface. She had finally been a real part of something. Something that mattered. They had to save Sam and it pained her to think they no longer needed or wanted her there.

"Marisa," Clairee said. "You died. In the past and the present! You were in the hospital. Between Beige and myself, we know your story. There's no reason for you to be here and put yourself at further risk. If anyone should be angry, it's us. You are showing a serious lack of concern for your health and as people who love you - that's not OK!"

"Clairee! I thought you of all people would want me here. Don't you want to do everything possible to save your son?"

"I have lived my life trying to find a way to save my son." She looked at Sam with such tenderness in her eyes that Marisa had to look away. "But I couldn't live with myself and I know Sam couldn't either if something were to happen to you because of that quest. You are family, Marisa."

"In more ways than one," Lilah piped up. "Remember Daddy says she's a Reece!"

"Rafe's here, too?" Marisa felt hurt all over again.

"Seriously Ris," Beige said, "We love you. You shouldn't be a part of this."

"I agree," said Sam.

"What about you, Ethan?" she asked. "What do you think?"

He looked at her and hung his head, "I think it's dangerous, Marisa, and I can't bear the thought of you going through anything else."

She felt the color rising in her cheeks.

"But," he continued, "I know how important this is to you, and I would never try and stop you from what you feel called to do."

She leaned in to snuggle at his side.

"Thank you," she said and smiled up at him.

"That doesn't mean I'm happy you're here," he said and scooted away.

"Would everybody stop being mad at each other?" Lilah yelled. "You guys are so stupid sometimes."

"Lilah!" Clairee said.

"Listen, I'm the one that had the vision about Ethan being hypnotized and I'm the one who can see my dad, and I know that none of it can happen without Marisa!"

Marisa watched Lilah jumping from one foot to the other as she talked. She was a bundle of energy tonight.

"You've got to be here, Marisa. You have to cast the spell! The protection spell will keep Sam safe while Dad helps him get Ethan hypnotized."

"Lilah, I'm hypnotizing Ethan," Clairee said. "Sam doesn't know how to do any of this."

"That's why Dad's gonna help him!" Lilah practically shouted.

"I think we need to cut back on her caffeine level," Sam joked.

Marisa watched Ethan's eyes ping pong from Clairee to Lilah to Sam. She knew he was confused and uncertain and it had only been a few days since she had promised not to use her spells on him.

"Ethan, this spell Lilah says I need to do, it's not a spell on you."

He turned to her. "I know, Marisa. It's a protection spell, like she said. I'm not sure what's happening here but I know that I can help. I want to go back. I want to help Sam. I need you to do the spell. I don't think I could trust that I'd be safe if you didn't."

She leaned over to kiss his cheek.

"Cut it out," Sam teased.

"Like I haven't dealt with enough PDA to last a lifetime from you and Beige," she replied. "At least my kiss was on the cheek."

"OK, children." Clairee emphasized the word. "We have work to do. Lilah, we need to know the plan. I'm assuming your father has one?"

Marisa watched as Lilah gave instructions like a little drill sergeant. She liked seeing her in charge. There was something natural about it, despite her eleven year-old body.

"Marisa, you cast the circle around Momma, Sam, and Ethan. Momma will do the ring and Sam will do Daddy's part," Lilah ordered.

"What do I do?" Beige asked.

"We just watch today, Beige. Our stuff will come later."

Marisa wondered how much Lilah knew but was holding back about their future. She seemed so confident that they could save her brother. Still, one thing at a time was all she could handle so she focused her energies on the circle.

"Are the candles and herbs I need in the shop?" she asked Clairee.

"They should be; I just restocked," Clairee responded.

Marisa walked to the other room. Her eyes scanned the shelves behind the register looking for the barberry root. A warm hand landed on her shoulder and squeezed.

"Can I help?"

Ethan's voice, soft and strong. Her favorite sound in the world. She slowly turned around into his chest and he held her in his arms. She relaxed into him and took a minute to breathe.

"Everything's going to be OK, Marisa. I'll be under your protection. Nothing can hurt me when I'm with you."

A disturbing thought surfaced from her memory. "When we were together in the past, I felt the same way. You told me not to worry, that you could heal me. But you couldn't. You couldn't here, either. What if I can't protect you, Ethan?"

He lifted her chin and kissed her softly. She loved the way his hands held her face, like it was some delicate piece of china.

"From what I gathered in there, the protection spell isn't for me. I'm only getting hypnotized. All I have to do is remember things."

"You're right. The spell is for Sam. He'll be connecting with his dad. I hope he can handle it."

"I don't think there's much Sam can't handle," Ethan said.

Marisa stood back and started loading candles into his arms. "You better be careful, Ethan Martos, that sounded like you just gave Sam a compliment."

"Not a compliment, really, but maybe the guy's OK."

She pointed towards the parlor, "March! One candle along the center of each wall. Clairee has the lighter." She grabbed the barberry root and followed him. It would all be OK. It had to be.

Chapter Thirty-Two

Sam couldn't believe what was happening. His father, the man he loved more than anyone else in the world. The one person who loved him more than anyone else ever had, sat on the opposite side of the room watching the preparations. From the moment Lilah told them that Sam would be doing the hypnosis with his father's help, he had been filled with an incredible sense of hope.

Would he finally feel his father's touch or hear the sound of his voice? Eyes so much like his own stared back at him, filled with love and pride. He could only imagine what they were trying to say. How was this going to work if he couldn't hear him? Why could his dad communicate with Lilah and not him?

Clairee finished lighting the candles and his father stepped inside as Marisa closed the circle. His father stood opposite him at the candle positioned to the North. That was right, Sam thought. He's our true north. He will guide me to my destiny, to where I need to be. He's what will bring me home.

Clairee was the East and Marisa the West. Ethan meanwhile was positioned in the center of the circle facing Clairee. Sam heard Marisa begin a low, quiet chant and he felt the air in the room take on a charge that hadn't been there before. It pulsed inside of him and connected him to each member of the circle. He could feel his mother's anxiety, Marisa's concentration, Ethan's anticipation, and his father's outpouring of love and confidence in him.

Clairee stepped forward.

"Ethan, as you watch my ring, I need you to focus on your breathing. Take long deep breaths in and then slowly release them. As you do, I'll take you through the steps to relax the muscles in your body. When we finish you will be in a state of total peace. Are you ready to begin?"

Sam saw Ethan nod. He tried to quell his own anxiety at not knowing what would happen. He trusted his father would show him at the right time, but it would have been nice to have practiced. He heard Clairee begin the instructions for Ethan. It was starting. What would his part entail? He looked at his father, who motioned him forward. They stepped inward towards Ethan. It was like walking towards himself in a mirror.

When he reached Ethan's side, he followed his father's lead and placed a hand on his shoulder. He could hear Clairee's voice clearly end the relaxation instructions. He wasn't sure how he knew what to do but he began to slowly count backwards from one hundred. With each number the world around him seemed to disappear. The light dimmed and reality faded until only his father remained. When he reached the end, everyone and everything was gone. Ethan was no longer between them. The shoulder he was holding was his dad's and his dad's hand gripped his own.

He clearly heard his father's voice in his mind.

"Sam, my Sam. Do you know how long I've watched and waited for this moment?"

So many emotions filled his body that he thought he might collapse from the chaos. He didn't know how to release it. The love and longing was overwhelming.

"Dad," was all he could manage to say.

"You are everything I hoped you would be, Sam."

Feelings broke free from their physical prison and tears rolled down his cheeks. He hadn't known how much he needed or wanted to hear those words. Since the day his father left this world he had hoped he was doing everything right. Taking care of Lilah and Clairee had been his whole life, until Beige of course. The weight of his father's hand on his shoulder was like a lifeline sending love, purpose, and approval directly into his soul.

"We can do this. Sam. Together, as a family. We can break this curse."

"How? Tell me what to do?" he begged as the intensity of the experience began to settle and the wonder began to take over.

"First we need to save you. There's a way to stop your death."

"Stopping my death won't break the curse?" he asked.

He watched his father slowly shake his head. His eyes filled with what looked like sadness.

"Breaking the curse involves all of you, including Beige, Ethan, and someone else. Someone you despise." His father looked sad. "Someone I know you won't want to work with."

A sharp pain of recognition rushed through from his hand, up his arm, to his chest.

"Sara."

"Yes, Sam. You'll need Sara to truly break the curse."

"But Dad," he began.

"Shhh...there's more important things to say. Don't dwell on your hatred, Sam. Hatred is weakness and you need your full strength to go on living. You'll need every ounce of your being to protect the ones we love."

He saw his father glance into the emptiness surrounding them as if looking for someone.

"Lilah," he said.

"She'll need you, Sam. You're her only hope."

He watched as his father's image began to shimmer in waves.

"What's happening? Why are you fading away?" He tried to keep the fear from his voice.

His father stepped closer and Sam felt his arms surround him in a tight embrace.

"You know what you need to know. I'm finished, Sam."

"No!" he cried. "I need you. You can't go. I love you, Dad." He tried to hold on tighter but with each movement his father's essence seemed to evaporate in front of him.

He heard his dad's voice one last time, "Choose love, Sam."

A bright flash illuminated every corner of the room. Clean white light lit the figures of Beige and Lilah huddled together outside the circle, Marisa and Clairee in deep meditation, and Ethan sitting motionless in the center of it all.

Somehow Sam knew that they all had experienced something different in the short amount of time they'd been under the spell. He hoped that perhaps everyone held a different piece to the puzzle and by pooling their experiences they could stop the curse's progression. He couldn't bring himself to contemplate his actual death, and his father had given him all the hope he needed to believe it wouldn't come to that.

His eyes adjusted to the candlelight surrounding him, and he heard Marisa's chant, quiet and consistent in the background. Clairee's voice signaled he had a job to do.

"Ethan, when you hear Sam reach a count of ten you'll wake from your rest. You'll feel energetic and refreshed. You'll remember everything that happened, but you won't feel any of the trauma or pain that accompanied the events. It will all be just an objective memory."

Sam saw her look his way, so he began to count.

"One...two...three..."

He watched Ethan's body begin to tremble and shake. Something wasn't right. This wasn't relaxed and refreshed.

"Four, five, six," he counted faster as the shaking increased to violent convulsions and Ethan's body fell from the chair to the floor.

"Seven, eight, nine, ten," he raced to the end knowing that Marisa had to close the spell and break the circle before Ethan could be helped.

Everything happened at once: as Marisa stopped chanting, Clairee rushed to Ethan's side, and Marisa and Lilah engulfed him in relieved hugs. The hugs were short lived when they realized that Ethan wasn't moving. He hadn't woken up.

Sam covered Lilah's ears as Marisa's tortured scream filled the room.

Chapter Thirty-Three

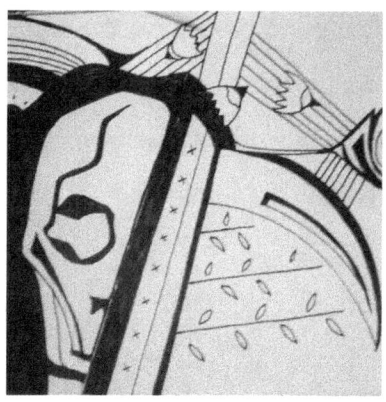

At first Ethan hadn't known where he was, but as he adjusted to the scene that surrounded him, he was able to pick out certain landmarks that told him he was still in Garrison. A light wind pushed his hair from his forehead and moved the branches surrounding him so that he recognized, not more than a mile away, the steeple of the church he attended with his family. But when he thought of his family a jumble of unfamiliar faces converged in his mind. He looked down and noticed his feet. The black laced boots weren't his Adidas and the coarse brown cotton of the pants was as strange as the boots. He never wore anything but jeans and soccer shorts.

It must have worked. The realization came to him quickly and he pressed his back to the outside wall of the small cabin where he stood. He listened for voices in his head. Somehow, he had expected to be guided in this journey through his past life. Hadn't Clairee said she'd be with him? There was nothing but the sounds of birds and the call of crickets. In the distance he thought he heard water. Maybe he was near the creek?

He edged his way down the side of the cabin, afraid to step into open space for fear of who he may encounter. Besides knowing his name was Michael, he didn't know much else about his life with Nora. When he came to a window in the cabin wall he carefully glanced inside. There, on the table in the center of the room was a body.

He pressed himself tighter against the wall. Marisa's body. It had to be. The cabin, the table, it was exactly as she'd described it. He was outside of the cabin where the woman he loved lay dying. Through the window he saw the door to the cabin slowly open a crack and a woman with olive skin and long dark hair tiptoed into the room.

Could that be Leila? Had Michael watched as she poisoned Nora?

He saw the woman touch Nora's face and put something to her lips. A feeling of utter helplessness fluttered through his nervous system. He could feel what Michael felt, he could even access his thoughts but he couldn't control what was happening. He wanted with all he had to go into the cabin and at least try to heal her. The poison hadn't been in her long enough to kill her, he knew Michael still had a chance, but instead he watched from the inside as the young man's heart broke wide open.

A small voice tugged at his consciousness. He heard the words, "follow her" quite clearly so when Leila left the cabin he did just that. He didn't know if the command came from Clairee or from

Michael himself but he crept after her, staying directly behind the treeline on the path.

She moved quickly through the woods with a sense of purpose, clutching something tightly to her chest. It was a peculiar size and made of paper but he couldn't quite catch a good look. While Ethan obviously picked up on its importance, Michael only wanted to see where she was headed.

When she emerged from the woods onto a small dirt road recognition coursed through his veins. Ethan had been there just days before. It was paved and lined with trees and houses in the future but there was no mistaking the familiar mansion Leila walked towards.

She stopped suddenly and looked around. Had she heard him? He stepped behind a large pine and watched her backtrack towards the woods. She turned full circle, searching for any onlookers. Finally satisfied she was alone, she removed a small metal case from her satchel. She placed the rectangular paper in the box. As she did, he caught a quick glimpse of the figure of a man with a scythe reaping human heads alongside what looked like shafts of wheat.

Leila dug a hole beneath the giant tulip poplar that Ethan knew still stood on Sara's street and buried the box, covering the hole with dirt and leaves. Calmly, she walked around to the back of the Smith estate where a gated white picket fence seemed to go on for acres. He dashed to the side of the house and hid by a large prickly rosebush that was shedding the last blooms of fall.

Leila knocked on the door.

A man's voice answered.

"Is it finished?"

"Yes," he heard her say.

"Did you bring the card?"

"It's safe. You promise this will keep him alive?" she asked.

Even with Ethan using the full force of his will, Michael wouldn't budge from behind that bush. Ethan needed to see the man. He had to know if it was Elliot. Michael's confusion and anger ripped through him. He too, wanted to see the man, to know who had ordered the death of his lover and what was so important about this card Leila buried with such fierce secrecy, but he stayed beside the house and listened instead.

"The cards control the curse. You've done as I asked and this cycle of the curse has been satisfied. Michael won't be harmed."

He heard a thump and risked a glance only to see Leila's crumpled figure on the ground, her shoulders racked with sobs.

"Get up, witch. This is what you wanted. Michael is safe and your competition is eliminated. You'll be a Lowell before you know it. Now, hand over the card and go back to your heathen family."

"This card, this curse, everything to do with it is evil," she spat at him. "Including, you, Eli!"

"Perhaps, but the soul that possesses the Noblet deck holds great power, witch. You of all people should know that, since your family imbued it," the man said.

"Then you should know that I of all people can destroy the cards and this curse," she hissed at him.

"While I wouldn't mind seeing the curse abolished, I have no reason to fear for my descendants as long as the deck is mine. Give me the card to make it whole again, Leila. I wouldn't test me, if I were you."

Ethan saw a hand reach out and grab Leila by the shoulder and pull her forward.

"The card, Leila. It doesn't belong to you. It needs to be kept in a safe place so it can't hurt anyone for another seventeen years. You think that by destroying that one card, you destroy the curse?"

"It's the only way," she said. "The only way to protect our children, and our children's children."

If you've destroyed that card, Leila, you won't any have children. Michael won't live out the day. I don't need magic to hurt him, you know. Only power, and I have plenty of that."

Ethan felt himself moving forward and out of the bushes.

Eli pulled Leila from the ground with one hand, his face inches from hers, seething. In his eyes was the closest thing to true hatred Ethan had ever seen.

"Shit!" he thought to himself, what had Michael done?

"Leave her alone," he heard himself yelling.

The man turned to face him. His hair was whiter but the wiry build was the same. Ethan looked into the sinister eyes of Elliot Smith.

"This young woman is responsible for the death of the girl you love. She killed her with a poison both sweet and vile." He turned to look at her, "Very reminiscent of the love and jealousy that rule your heart, Leila. If you'd only been able to make decisions with your brain instead, you might have lived."

"She doesn't have the card," Michael said. "I do."

Ethan could hardly believe what was coming out of his mouth. Why would he want to help the woman who had killed his Nora? Not only that, but he had to know he was putting his own life at risk.

"There's been enough death, Eli. Let her go and I'll lead you to it."

Michael's eyes caught Leila's and the feeling of fear overwhelmed him and compressed his heart, making it hard to breathe. Ethan recognized the emotions instantly. She was his friend. He didn't want her to die. He had to help her. She'd killed Nora, but he loved her, too, in an entirely different way.

"He's lying." Leila said. She stood tall and proud. "He doesn't have the card. I've destroyed it."

Ethan watched as Eli took another step towards Leila, his hands wrapping tightly around her throat. It all happened so quickly he almost didn't have time to comprehend exactly what took place. He felt Michael's hand reach into his pocket and pull out something sharp and cold. He was suddenly rushing the man with a dagger bared in anger with murderous intent.

Eli pushed Leila to the ground and turned in time to catch Michael's hand that held the dagger. With a strength unnatural for a body so old, Eli somehow managed to turn the dagger towards him. The blade buried itself in Michael's chest in one quick clean movement. The sharp pain convulsed his body, and Ethan could feel fear and anger as he struggled in vain for breath. He looked towards Leila, willing her to run, but the last thing he saw was Eli's hands around her throat and the glint from the green gemstone on the dagger in his chest.

Chapter Thirty-Four

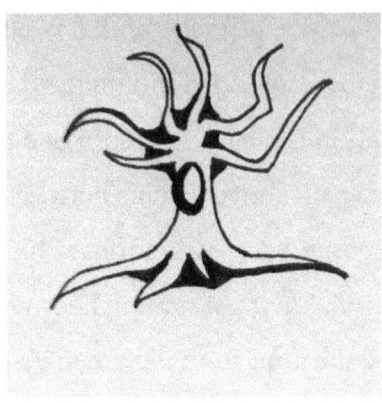

"Why won't he wake up?" Marisa looked from Clairee back to Beige. "Do your cards. See if he's OK. Somebody do something."

Clairee moved towards her and wrapped her arm around Marisa's shoulders.

"Give him time, Marisa. He's back with us, just not completely yet. His mind needs time to heal from the trauma of what he experienced when he was under."

Marisa looked at the handsome, athletic boy lying on the small parlor couch that Sam had moved him to as soon as she'd opened the circle.

"I couldn't protect him. It's obvious he was in pain. Why couldn't I help him?"

"You know the protection spell wasn't for him, Marisa." Sam said. "It was for me. It let me connect with my dad so that we could take Ethan back." He pulled her close to thank her. "You gave me my last chance to feel my father's love."

She let him hug her. She knew what it had meant for Sam to communicate with Rafe, and she knew the purpose of her spell, but why couldn't it have helped Ethan, too? Protection was protection, damn it.

"You would think whoever had been in the circle should have been fine," she pulled away and looked to Clairee

"We don't know that it didn't protect him, Marisa. The way his body was thrashing on the floor, he obviously underwent something extremely painful. Who's to say that without your spell the effects of the trauma might have crossed over with him. Look what happened when you died as Nora."

"That was magic, Clairee."

"This was magic, too, Marisa. My husband and son were able to hold each other across dimensions in order to take Ethan back to a memory of a time and a place we didn't even know about a month ago. Don't minimize what occurred in this parlor. It was magical and dangerous."

"He's moving!" Lilah cried.

Marisa looked to the couch and saw Ethan's head turn from side to side. He raised his arm and rubbed his chest before opening his eyes and yawning. She was down on her knees with her head on his chest before he had time to speak.

"Hi there," he said. He lifted her hair from his face. "No fair trying to suffocate me with hair after what I've just been through."

He laughed, but she couldn't. She could feel the tears threatening to spill any second.

Clairee came up behind her. "May I?"

Marisa stepped aside as Clairee checked his pupils and felt his forehead for signs of fever.

"Do I pass the test, Mom?"

Clairee ruffled his brown sweaty curls. "I don't know if I can handle another son, Ethan, but yes, I think you'll be fine."

He slowly sat up, again reaching for his chest as if checking to make sure it was still there. Marisa sat next to him, curling into his side and snuggling as tightly as she could against him.

He looked down at her and pressed his lips to her forehead.

"I'm OK. Really, I made it back and I'm fine."

"Are you sure?" Her eyes searched his.

"Didn't you just get finished bragging that you have a boyfriend who doesn't lie?"

"I think she did, yes," Beige chimed in. "I hate to be the one to bring us back to business, but I happen to have a boyfriend who seems to be the target of a curse. Ethan, did you find out anything? Anything at all that we can use?"

Marisa watched Ethan look at Sam.

"Sam, my friend...I think after this you're gonna owe me big time," Ethan said.

"What does that mean, Ethan?" Clairee asked.

"The curse is definitely connected to the cards."

"Just like Daddy said, Momma!"

"Lilah - shhh! What cards? What did Rafe know when he died?"

228

"I can't answer that for sure, but I can make a guess," Ethan said. "It turns out that the curse itself is controlled by a certain deck that your family saturated in magic, Clairee. He called it the Noblet. I don't know what that means but that's what he said."

"Who's he?" Sam asked.

"Eli Smith. Shares an uncanny resemblance to Sara's dad, somehow," Ethan replied.

"So, Sara's family has had the cards all along," Sam said. "Another strike against Sara." He looked at Beige.

"There's so much wrong with that statement, Sam, I'm not sure where to begin," Ethan said. "But let's start with the fact that while Mr. Smith and his family may have been in possession of the athame, they haven't had the full Noblet deck since at least 1911."

"What do you mean, Ethan?" Clairee asked.

Marisa watched as Ethan struggled to put what he remembered into words.

"Leila, the girl responsible for Nora's death, killed Nora to protect Michael." He squeezed Marisa's hand. "Her vision wasn't about you, it was about me, and she used the card from the Noblet deck to substitute your death as a Reece, for mine."

"But that's crazy!" Beige said.

Marisa held tightly to his hand as he continued.

"Michael saw her kill Nora and he followed her to the Smith estate."

"That's where I lost you," Clairee interrupted. "I told you to follow her and then suddenly you were gone. I couldn't make contact."

"That was the last I heard from you, too." Ethan said. She was carrying something against her chest the whole way. It was the card she'd gotten from Eli Smith. I tried to see it. Best I could tell it was the figure of a man with a scythe."

"The Death card. It looks slightly different in that deck than it does today," Clairee said. "Tell me the girl was smart enough not to give the card back to Eli Smith. You said they no longer have a full deck in their possession."

"She buried it," he said.

"And you know where!" Marisa said, suddenly jumping to her feet. "If we have that card, we can control the curse. We can save Sam."

Beige fell into Sam's arms.

Lilah started jumping up and down, "We did it! We did it," she chanted.

Only Clairee and Ethan remained silent.

"As long as the card is still where Leila buried it, we've saved Sam and we do control the curse," Clairee held up her hand to quiet the group, "but..."

"As long as the curse exists, it still demands a victim from one of the three families," Ethan concluded. "We not only have the power to save Sam's life, we hold the power to take the life of someone else, and that's not a power any human being should hold," Ethan said.

"I don't know about that," Sam chimed in. "I have a few ideas for who the curse could take out."

"Stop it, Sam!" Clairee yelled at him.

Marisa had never heard Clairee yell. And yell she did. "Have you learned nothing? Nothing at all from what we've been through this past year? How dare you wish the feelings of helplessness and despair that you've been saddled with onto that poor girl, no matter what you think she did."

Marisa watched Sam's face change from anger to shame.

"I'm sorry, Mom. You're right."

Clairee looked confused. Marisa thought it was because Sam so rarely admitted he was wrong.

"Later, when we've all had a chance to rest and recover from today, I'll tell you what Dad had to say. But for now, at least, just know that I know I have to change. Hatred won't break this curse."

"And that's what we're going to do now," Marisa said as she looked at Ethan and smiled. "We're going to break this curse. All of us. Together.

Sneak Peek: Book Three of The Sacrificial Fortunes Series

Dead quiet surrounded him as he broke the damp earth with his small shovel. Only a few beams of moonlight lit the area under the giant, shedding tulip poplar on the quiet street lined with large homes and estates.

"Hurry up!" she whispered. "I see headlights."

He grabbed for her hand and pulled her behind the wide trunk, out of view from the passing vehicle.

"If this weren't a matter of life and death I could get really distracted right now, Marisa," he said, holding her in his arms, pressed against the trunk.

"We could be done with this so much quicker if you'd let me do a cloaking spell instead of making us hide behind a tree," she said.

"I love that you're a good witch, and one day I might be totally comfortable with your spells and even my healing abilities, but right now I think using magic might be a little dangerous," Ethan said.

He stepped from their hiding spot and knelt, continuing the small hole already in progress. He had no idea if the metal box containing the missing card from the Noblet tarot deck could have survived a hundred years in its shallow grave, but he hoped for the sake of Marisa, their future, and the lives of their family and friends it was still there.

"I don't think Elliot Smith can smell magic, Ethan. He's human, not some mystical hound dog," Marisa said stepping back into her spot as sentry and crossing her arms.

"Elliot Smith is more than you or Beige could possibly imagine, Marisa. I'm not sure what he's capable of, but since he's killed me once, I'm not willing to take any chances," Ethan said.

The memory of his past life regression just hours before, was still fresh in his mind. He could feel the slice of cold steel breaking the skin of his chest and the helplessness that had overwhelmed him as he watched Leila Denoncourt strangled.

"We don't know if the Eli Smith in your regression was Elliot or not, Ethan. I mean, look at me. I looked nothing like Nora but I was definitely her in my past life," Marisa said. "Just because he resembled him doesn't make Sara's dad the man who killed you. It was a past life and they're from the same gene family...of course they'd share some features."

"I don't know how to explain this to you, Marisa," he said. The frustration mounted in his chest, and he wiped sweat from his brow despite the chilly night. Only four days remained until Samhain, or Halloween as he'd called it up until about two weeks ago. "It's a feeling. I sat in Mr. Smith's den the other day and stared the man down. I challenged him about how your athame got into the shipment at Fortunes. He didn't threaten me with words, but it was the same feeling I felt when Michael stood before Eli Smith."

"I'm not saying you're wrong, Ethan. Only that we can't make assumptions with any of this," she said. "Are you almost done? It's getting cold."

He watched her shivering, slipped off his jacket, and threw it in her direction.

"If he's not Eli, then how do you explain why he made it a point to put that dagger, the one that killed me, into my hand last year? He wanted a reaction! He was testing me to see what I knew."

Vibrations reverberated up the bones in his hand and wrist as the shovel struck something hard. His breathing quickened and he closed his eyes, hoping with all he had that it was the box he'd watched Leila Denoncort bury in 1911.

"I think I've found something," he said, careful to keep the excitement out of his voice in case it was a tree root or some buried child's treasure from years past.

Marisa rushed to his side.

"Keep watching for people, Marisa! We can't be found out. Not when we have the advantage. No one knows what we know yet."

"Just pull it out already, Ethan! It's right there, I can see it." She pointed to the dirty metal corner peeking from the sunken dirt.

He submerged his hands in the wet, brown gunk, grabbed hold of metal and pulled. When it loosened easily doubts started looming. After a hundred years shouldn't it be harder to get out? Wouldn't the dirt have compacted? Wasn't it too close to the surface?

Marisa's voice interrupted, "Open it, Ethan. We have to know."

He lifted the small silver latch on the side of the box and used his thumbs to pry the top upward. He pressed harder, thinking years of rust and dirt might have sealed it more solidly than he thought. On the third attempt, when it wouldn't budge, he looked up at Marisa. Her long red curls danced on the cool night breeze.

"She was a Denoncourt, Ethan. That box is spelled," she said.

She reached out her hand to take it from him, but the lights from a distant car pierced the black of the street.

"Quick, behind the tree," she said.

In each other's arms once again, Ethan could feel Marisa's rapidly beating heart hold time with his own. What had he gotten himself into? Yes, he loved her. Almost losing her in the hospital a few weeks before had made that abundantly clear, but witches? Past lives? Tarot cards?

How did the kid who led the school mission trips, the kid who everyone thought might be a minister himself one day, end up working with a psychic and people who could talk to the dead? Still, when he held her in his arms, Ethan knew that no matter how strange and scary this new adventure was, he'd never go back to the life he led before he fell under the spell of this shy, sweet, loving girl.

"It's slowing down," she whispered as the sound of the engine approached.

"Just stay still. I've got the shovel. No one should notice a pile of overturned dirt under a tree," he said.

A car door shut gently, proving him wrong.

"Ethan!"

He recognized the hushed voice calling his name.

"Ethan! I know you're here," Beige said. "Clairee sent us. We've got to get you two out of here now. You're about to be discovered."

"Yeah, because you're idling a car on a deserted street and yelling my name at two a.m.," he said as he stepped from behind the tree, box in hand.

"Oh my God! You found it," Beige said and began jumping up and down.

"Shut up!" he snapped at her and then felt remorse. "What do you mean we're about to be discovered?" He waved to Sam in the driver's seat. It was still pretty new trying to be nice to the guy he'd disliked for so long.

Marisa pushed him from behind, "Get in the car, Ethan! Now."

He looked towards the Smith estate surrounded by its winding white picketed fence as far as the eye could see. A light that hadn't been there before illuminated a small window in the back of the home. Anyone looking from that window could easily see what was happening where they now stood.

"That's Sara's room," Beige said.

"Better than her father's," he replied.

The three of them squeezed quickly into Sam's back seat.

"Drive!" Ethan ordered.

Sam looked back at him before he put the car in gear, "You got it?" he asked.

"We got it," he said and handed the unopened box to Marisa who tried but had no luck opening it either.

She handed it to Beige.

"You try," she said. "Do you think Sara saw us? Is that why Clairee sent you guys? To get us before she could wake her dad?"

"I don't know. We were watching a movie, trying to relax from all the shit that went down tonight when mom burst into my room and said we had to go," Sam said.

"What are you two doing out here anyway? You didn't say a word about this! I thought you were all about us ending this curse by working together, Marisa?"

Beige sounded hurt, so Ethan spoke up.

"It wasn't her fault. I realized her mom thought she was staying with you and that there was no better time than the present to test out the truth from my regression. I couldn't get it out of my head anyway, so instead of taking her home and having her mom ask lots of questions we came here."

"And where were you planning to go after here?" Beige wiggled her eyebrows at Marisa.

"Nowhere Beige. I don't think we thought it through. It felt like what we needed to do," Marisa said.

"Take it from me," Sam called back. "Doing what feels right can get you into hot water."

Ethan thought Sam was referring to the way he'd handled the situation with Sara after Beige had been drugged. His secrecy about how he'd dealt with her and continued to protect Beige from her nearly destroyed their relationship.

"It all worked out, though. We don't know if Sara saw us or not, but if she did, I have a much better chance at handling her than her father," Ethan said.

Beige handed the box back to him.

"I give up. It won't budge."

"Marisa says the box is spelled. We'll need Clairee's help tomorrow, so why don't you take the box, Sam, drop me at my ca,r and I'll take the girls back to Beige's."

"At two a.m.?" Beige asked. "My mom thinks I'm at Marisa's."

"OK, well, what do you guys suggest? I told my parents I'd be staying at Tommy's because of an early soccer practice," Ethan said.

Beige gave him a shocked look.

"You lied?" She asked.

"I'm a changed man," he said. "Although, I'm not sure it's for the better."

Sam pulled the car into a 24 hour breakfast place. "Looks like our first all-nighter. Probably one of many more to come," he said.

"Only if that box contains the card we need to save you, Sam," Marisa warned.

"Way to be a downer, Ris," Beige said.

Kimmy L. Davis

ABOUT THE AUTHOR

Kimmy L. Davis is a writer of young adult and middle grade fiction who also works as a high school teacher in Louisville, KY. She holds a BA in Communications from Bellarmine University and is currently working on a Master of Educational Technology degree through Boise State. She is a member of the Society of Children's Book Writers and Illustrators.

When not teaching, Kimmy enjoys reading young adult, romance, and sci-fi novels and traveling with her 14 year-old niece. She loves technology, particularly Twitter and enjoys blogging on a variety of topics from personal relationships to reality television. If there's any time left over she dabbles in visual arts.

Follow her at Kimmyld67 on Twitter, or visit her websites at Kimmyldavis.com and Kimmyldavis.net. Please leave your reviews on Goodreads.com and Amazon.com.

www.ingramcontent.com/pod-product-compliance
Lightning Source LLC
Chambersburg PA
CBHW060132130626

46556CB00006B/2316